FALLON WALKER

Eldest Son of an Eldest Son

First edition

ISBN: 9798570460492

Editing by Cassandra Faustini
Cover art by Primrose Woolcott
Cover art by Matthew Smaglik

This book was professionally typeset on Reedsy.
Find out more at reedsy.com

Contents

To my mom and to people who get lost in stories.

1

Chapter 1

Once upon a time…

There was a great kingdom, built on prophecy, legend, and great feats of bravery. One such legend stated that on the birthdate of every future king, the eldest son of an eldest son, rain would fall on a cloudless day. And the legend proved true for centuries.

Until King Cederic's eldest child was born.

King Cederic sat on a stone bench in the castle's innermost courtyard. His wife, Queen Belinda, was inside, giving birth to their first child, and Cederic was finding it difficult to concentrate on anything until his wife and new child were safe.

Elsewhere, his advisors stared at the sky, waiting to see if the queen had given them an heir. Miles and miles away, a young wizard named Dwennon watched the sky as well.

The king stood up and began pacing. He circled the little courtyard, weaving in and out of the trees. Then, he felt a raindrop. He tilted his head up to the sunny sky and smiled as another drop tapped him on the forehead.

The king's advisors murmured in excitement, shaking each other's hands, as if they'd had something to do with the birth.

Dwennon stuck his hand out and felt the soft rain falling from the cloudless sky.

The kingdom rejoiced. But the celebration ended abruptly when it was discovered that the queen had not given birth to a boy. Queen Belinda had given birth to a girl, who would never sit on the throne.

The king consulted with all manner of clerics and wise men and wizards, demanding an answer. Why had the rain fallen while the sun shone when he'd been given a daughter?

Two of these supposed wisemen gathered in the throne room. They wilted under the power of the king's furious gaze.

"Well?" the king demanded, "What answer have you?"

There was silence, until the wizard, named Craic, finally stepped forward. "Some sort of error," he said, "these things do happen from time to time."

"An error,' the king said. "Do the gods often make errors?"

The cleric, Jord, came forward. "Well, not so much an error, as a cosmic mixup."

"And what, pray tell, does that mean?" the king said, his voice low and dangerous.

The two wisemen glanced at each other.

Jord started strong but became too nervous to finish. "It means..."

"It means that surely all will be set to rights when the queen gives birth to a son. An actual son," Craic said.

The king was not heartened by this news. "Get out."

"Sire-" Craic said.

"Out!" the king roared. He picked up a heavy metal cup and launched it at Craic's head. The cup bounced off the wizard's forehead. "Get out!"

Being wise men, they did as the king asked.

Later, they stopped at a tavern for a moment before repairing back to their respective homes. They each ordered an ale and then sat down at a table.

Craic daubed at his forehead with an ink stained handkerchief. "That went very poorly."

"So sorry to hear that," a man at a table behind the wizard said. He sat with his back facing them, so all they could see was his long dark hair.

"Are you speaking to us?" Jord said.

"Of course," the man said. "So sorry things didn't go well with the king."

"How do you know we were meeting with the king? Who are you?" Craic asked.

"Terribly rude of me to eavesdrop, but I just couldn't resist," the man said. He turned around to face the two wise men.

"Dwennon," Craic said, not sounding particularly pleased to see the younger wizard.

"You know this man?" Jord asked.

"Unfortunately," Craic said. Even among the notoriously eccentric wizards, Dwennon was considered odd.

"Have you been invited to consult with the king?" Jord asked.

Craic snorted in laughter. "Of course not. The king would never consult with him. He's no one."

Dwennon did not seem bothered by the older wizard's insult. "He is, of course, right. I have not had the honor of offering my thoughts on the birth of the royal child."

"Your thoughts?" Craic asked. "What thoughts could you possibly have? I suppose you think it was fairies, or a curse, or the gods having a laugh."

"Oh, nothing so exciting," Dwennon said. "Perhaps the reason you can't find a magical answer, is because the answer is actually quite mundane."

"And what might this mundane reason be?" Craic asked.

"Perhaps the reason that the rains fell on a sunny day is that the queen gave birth to a son."

Jord and Craic both roared with laughter. Dwennon took no offense, just waited for them to tire themselves out.

Finally Craic got himself back under control. "Oh Dwennon, you do make me laugh. Surely you cannot be so stupid. You know what a girl is. You know what a boy is."

Dweenon shrugged and took a long swig of his drink.

"You'll see. The queen will give birth to a boy. The unclouded rains will fall again and all this bad business will be behind us," Jord said.

Dwennon had his doubts.

Those doubts were proven out several years later, when the queen did give birth to a son. The skies did not open for him.

The king's eldest child, though born a girl, felt in his heart that he was truly

3

a boy, his father's eldest son, and rightful heir to the throne. He refused to answer to his given name and would only allow himself to be called Allard, after Allard of the Green, the greatest knight in the history of the realm.

When Allard was six, he stood in the center of his pretty bedroom with the painted flowers on the walls and the dusty rose furniture. He clamped his arms to his sides. His nanny tried to pry his arms up so that she could put him in the dress that some duchess or another had sent as a birthday gift.

"Come along, princess. It's such a pretty dress."

Allard ducked his head down so his long blonde hair fell in his face.

"Well, you can't wear that," Nanny said. She gestured at the breeches and loose linen shirt he wore.

Nanny once again tried to prise his arms from his sides, but Allard used all his strength to keep his arms down.

"You are being a very rude little girl," Nanny said. "You'll take those clothes off, wear this dress, and I won't hear another word about it."

Allard's cheeks burned. He hated to be rude. But on this point, he could not budge.

Nanny grabbed his face, squeezing his cheeks, forcing him to look her in the eye. "Princess-"

"Allard," he said. "My name is Allard."

"No. It isn't. Your name is-"

"Allard!" he screamed. "My name is Allard!"

Nanny's face fell slack with shock. The royal child was generally very sweet and easily cowed if she sensed someone getting upset.

"My name is Allard!" he screamed again.

"What on earth is going on in here?" Queen Belinda said as she entered the room.

Allard turned to his mother, "Please mama, please make them listen."

"She's just having a tantrum, your majesty. Doesn't want to wear a dress," Nanny said.

Allard clenched his fists, waiting for the queen's pronouncement. He could defy his nanny, and the other members of the court, maybe even his father. But he couldn't defy his mother.

"Then she won't," the queen said easily. "Allard is just a child. It matters not."

Allard ran forward and buried his face in his mother's skirts, hugging around her legs.

"Very well, your majesty. Come Princess-" Nanny began.

"Allard, everyone shall call him Allard," the queen commanded.

Nanny nodded. "Very good ma'am." She gritted her teeth. "Come along… Allard."

King Cederic was not well pleased. He told his wife so, that night as they laid together in bed.

"You may rule out there," the Queen said, "but when it comes to our children, my word is law." Then she made a grotesque face at him to cut the tension, which never failed to make Cederic laugh. Her husband kissed her and there was no more talk of Allard's name.

When Allard was 9 years old, he was jolted out of bed by screams outside his window. There were several loud crashes and horrible screeching so loud it echoed in his ears. He whipped open the curtain that covered his window. The one that overlooked the courtyard.

A gigantic eye, vivid glittering green with a black vertical slit, always dancing with chilling good cheer, was outside his window. The eye was bigger than Allard's entire body. Allard screamed and backed away from the window.

A deep rumbling voice shook the walls of Allard's room and drove him to his knees."Ahhhhh. Helllllloooooooo little prince," a voice drawled lazily. The eye darted around in its socket, looking the room over. It tilted up at the corner, as if its owner was smiling at some private cruel joke.

The eye was replaced by the creature's mouth, a large cavern filled with teeth that reached all the way down the esophagus to the stomach, lit by a floating ball of fire at the back of the throat. A dragon.

"You look positively…delicious."

The dragon's gigantic forked tongue snaked in through the window and wrapped around Allard's ankle. The dragon's tongue was so hot it seared Allard's skin. It knocked him off his feet and started dragging him toward the window, where the dragon's mouth awaited.

Allard screamed and scrambled for the secret practice sword he kept under his bed. But he couldn't reach it. And as he got closer to the window, the air grew hotter and hotter.

His bedroom door crashed open. Queen Belinda ran into the room wielding an old sword. With a scream loud enough to make her voice crack, she stabbed the sword into the dragon's tongue, pinning it to the floor, and causing it to release its grip on Allard's ankle. His ankle was badly burnt, and he would have a scar all his life.

The dragon ripped his tongue in twain, pulling it past the blade until it was once again free. He flew off, and Allard launched himself into his mother's arms, sobbing.

Belinda held him close for a moment, but only for a moment. They were not yet out of danger. Dragons could heal quickly and she'd only done enough damage to make this one angry. He would be back.

"Alright my darling. We have to get out of here. We'll grab your brother and go to the cliffs," the queen said.

They grabbed Allard's brother, Braxton, then only 5 years old, and raced through the main hall until they reached the entrance to the tunnels. The tunnels led to a set of stairs embedded in the cliffside that led down to a canyon where they would be safe.

They had nearly reached the entrance to the tunnel when the dragon crashed through the ceiling of the great hall. He was too large to fit his entire body in the room, so he stuck his head and neck through a hole to lunge at Allard, his brother, and the queen from above.

The Queen was able to deflect him a couple times with the sword, but then the blade got stuck in the dragon's thick hide. The dragon pulled his head back through the hole in the ceiling and took the sword with him, ripping it from her hands. So she grabbed Allard's hand and ran back the way they came, but the dragon punched his claws through the roof and snagged her and her children.

With two great beats of the dragon's wings, they were airborne.

Allard had never seen anything so big in his life. Just one of the dragon's wings was the size of a sail on his father's largest ship. Allard opened his mouth to scream, but his screams were stolen by the wind whipping his face. He looked down to see his mother desperately clinging to Braxton.

Large fires dotted the castle. King Cederic's soldiers were arming the trebuchet on the highest defensive wall, trying desperately to hit the dragon before it got too far away. They fired, and a gigantic flaming ball of pitch and tar hurtled toward them and the dragon. It connected with the dragon's tail and the dragon nearly dropped them as he adjusted his flight path. The dragon swooped in back low over the defensive wall, spraying fire on the soldiers down below.

Allard's father stood on the bridge that led from the defensive walls to the main castle, wielding his sword.

"Balsinew!" King Cederic screamed, for the dragon was wiley Balsinew of the Glittering Eye, looking to add something new to his collection. "Let my wife and children go! It's me you want!"

"Hmmm." The sound of the dragon humming so close was loud enough to make Allard's ears and nose bleed. He covered his ears and his mother did her best to cover Braxton's.

The dragon landed on the bridge. Several of the supports cracked under his weight.

"Mmmmmighty presumptuous of you," the dragon said. But he did release his grip on the queen and Braxton. He kept his hold on Allard, however.

The king lunged forward. The dragon pretended to drop Allard, and Cederic froze. Then the dragon caught Allard and laughed. He waggled a claw in the king's direction. His eyes danced in the dark.

"I'd not move too quickly," the dragon said. A grin curled across his face. "I might startle, and then what would happen to the little prince?"

Allard moaned in fear but did not cry out. He would be brave.

Cederic turned to his wife. "Take Braxton and go. I'll get our child back."

Belinda shook her head. "I can't leave you. I can't leave him!" She reached longingly for Allard.

"We have to protect Braxton," Cederic said. "He is the future king."

The queen pointed at one of the soldiers, who was impossibly young, still a child. "You. Come here."

The soldier stepped forward. Queen Belinda shoved Braxton into the soldier's arms. "Take him to the tunnels. Keep him safe." This way she could get two children out of harm's way, Braxton and the young soldier.

The soldier looked to the king for confirmation. He nodded. "Go."

The king and queen refocused their attention on the dragon and Allard. Cederic stepped forward. "Give me my child."

"I don't think I will. I think I'll just eat him up right now," Balsinew said.

The dragon opened his mouth wide. The fireball at the back of his throat grew in size until it illuminated the night sky. He dangled Allard above his mouth like a cruel cat playing with a plump and delicious mouse.

"No!" the queen screamed.

Allard didn't dare kick or struggle, lest he cause the shirt he was hanging by to rip and send him tumbling down the dragon's gullet.

The dragon lowered Allard. "Then again…Maybe I won't."

With a scream, the king rushed forward, sword over his head, intent on plunging it straight into Balsinew's heart.

But the dragon easily knocked the king aside. Cederic slammed into a stone wall. The king tried to climb to his feet, but found that his legs would not respond to his commands. He struggled to move at all. He could only watch as the dragon swept the remaining soldiers off the bridge, leaving his wife and child with no defense.

The queen picked up the king's sword and ran forward. The dragon swiped at her and she managed to stab him in the arm. Then she stuck the sword in the dragon's great belly.

The dragon let out a pained roar so loud that for the rest of his life Allard would be sensitive to loud noises and have trouble hearing soft ones. The dragon let go of Allard, tossing him onto the bridge, and then he beat his giant wings and took flight. Dragons were patient creatures, always willing to disengage until they were sure they once again had the advantage.

Belinda stood Allard up and told him to go to his father. Allard wanted to refuse, wanted to protect his mother. His mother could sense this. But she needed him out of harm's way. Queen Belinda picked up an orphaned sword from where it lay next to its fallen owner; she swung it experimentally a few times. Then she nodded to herself. It would do.

"Mama," Allard said.

"I'll be alright." Belinda could hear the great flapping sound that meant the dragon was coming back. She kept the orphan sword for herself and gave the king's sword to Allard. "You go. Protect your king. And I'll do the same." The queen knew that the only way to get Allard to safety was to appeal to his sense of duty, his sense of honor.

Allard hesitated once more. Belinda gathered him in her arms and gave him a tight hug. "Go!"

Allard nodded and ran to his father's side. His father was unconscious, and so Allard had to drag him back into the castle.

A great crash sounded. The dragon had once again landed on the bridge, damaging it further. Allard pulled hard, trying to get his father inside to safety. Once he had his father situated in the entrance hall, he ran back outside, just in time to hear his mother's scream and see a great flash of light. The bridge broke under Queen Belinda's feet and she fell toward the water below.

The dragon snatched her out of the air.

Allard raced forward with his father's sword, determined to save his mother, though he had no idea how he could possibly reach her. In the end, he could only watch in horror as the dragon beat the air with his great wings and took off into the night sky with the queen clutched in his claws.

Allard never saw his mother again.

2

Chapter 2

The entire kingdom mourned for Queen Belinda, for she had been good and kind and brave and had helped her trophy-hunter husband ascend to something higher than the truly mediocre leader he would have been otherwise.

The king's greatest regret, the thing that haunted him, was that since the truncated fight with the dragon, he'd lost the use of his legs and could not pursue the dragon for revenge. He offered a reward for any that might bring him Balsinew's eye. But none had ever returned.

The castle, once a warm and happy place, grew cold and hostile. The best Allard could hope from his father was to be ignored, because whenever he was the subject of his father's focus, he was the focus of his father's displeasure. His father would complain about the way he dressed and the way he talked and how it was going to be next to impossible to find Allard a husband, which Allard was quite fine with. His father mostly focused on training Braxton to one day take the throne. Braxton was mostly interested in torturing the mice he trapped under his bed. Allard would always set the mice free, but Braxton could always find more.

So Allard mostly stayed out of his father and brother's way. He trained with the sword he wasn't supposed to have, and read of the great deeds of the kings of old in the books he'd been told were quite improper for a young lady.

A year after losing his mother, Allard had given up on the idea of ever smiling again, until a very strangely-dressed man arrived at the castle door, announcing that he'd been hired as Allard's etiquette teacher. This was strange for a number of reasons. The first was that he seemed to have just appeared inside the castle walls. Some children claimed they'd seen him floating over the trees and then he'd just floated into the inner hold of the fortress like-castle. The second reason was that no one remembered hiring an etiquette teacher for Allard, but when they went through their records they found it had indeed all been arranged.

The man wore a large black hat dotted with sparkling starlight, an emerald green cloak, and dark spectacles the likes of which the castle staff had never seen. He had long dark hair and a mouth that never seemed to quite stop smiling. He called himself Dwennon. Dwennon was shown to his young charge's quarters. The maid who guided Dwennon to Allard's room warned him that the eldest royal child was a bit strange, insisted on being called a boy. "But maybe you'll fix all that."

Dwennon had no intention of fixing "all that". He had much more interesting plans for Allard.

When Dwennon met Allard, the boy was drawing a battle plan for some toy soldiers he was not supposed to have. The toys were arranged in an elaborate battle sequence. At first the boy did not hear him approach; when Allard finally looked up, he made to shove the soldiers back into the box, but Dwennon held up his hand.

"Wait," he walked over and looked over the battle and Allard's plan. "Why not attack from this ridge?" Dwennon asked, pointing to a few soldiers standing at the edge of Allard's bed.

"We'd lose too many soldiers that way," Allard said. He looked down and drew a few more soldiers in the trees along the banks of the blanket river and then arranged them accordingly on the battlefield.

"What does it matter?" Dwennon asked. "They're just tin."

Allard's eyes flashed up to Dwennon. "They won't always be." He returned his attention to his battle plan.

Dwennon smiled. The boy was all he'd hoped for when he'd seen the unclouded rains, though quite serious for someone so young. He'd have to see if he could do anything about that. If there was no laughter in a ruler's heart, the weight of his great responsibility would crush him.

Over the next 11 years, Allard learned many things from Dwennon. State craft. Battle strategy. Basic defensive magic. Bawdy marching songs. Animal husbandry. Figure drawing. Public speaking. Irrigation. Sanitation. Mythology. Languages. Sword fighting. And Allard's great passion, cartography. Dwennon took Allard to visit battlefields to tend to the wounded, so he would understand the cost of war. He had Allard help a family put up hay for harvest so he understood backbreaking work. They visited jails and monasteries. They traveled to distant lands, where Allard learned the ways and customs of their neighbors near and far. Dwennon taught him so very many things. But they never did get around to etiquette. On that front, Allard needed no help.

As Allard grew older, he began taking "diplomatic trips" that no one seemed to know anything about. He would return with cuts and bruises on his face and person. And he wouldn't stop smiling for days afterward. When asked about these trips, he grew uncharacteristically elusive and would quickly change the subject.

One day, Dwennon followed him. The prince rode through the night to the next realm over, mostly keeping to the trees to avoid other riders on the main road. Dwennon soared over the trees to keep pace with him. Finally the prince arrived at his destination, a tournament. He put on his armor in the woods and then emerged to sign up to compete. He easily dominated in every category, but he never once removed his helmet during the entire competition.

After he was awarded his final trophy, he climbed on his horse and disappeared into the trees. He rode for a time and Dwennon silently followed. As a wizard, he was quite good at avoiding detection. He finally came upon Allard laboriously removing his armor in a small clearing, his handsome face bright red from the heat, his dirty blond hair sweat matted to his forehead.

"Why do you not remove your helmet?" Dwennon asked as he stepped out of the trees.

Allard jumped and then rolled his eyes and went back to removing his armor, quite a feat with no squire to help him. "Because I do not wish to shame my opponent," he said.

"And why would they be shamed?"

"Because they lost," Allard said. He worked at the buckles on his chest plate. He had to twist and bend to get at them.

"Someone always loses. The honor is in the attempt," Dwennon said.

"Because they lost to me."

"A formidable opponent?"

Allard sighed. He kept his eyes on his work. He knew where Dwennon was leading him. And he had little patience for it. He just wanted to get out of the hot armor and dive into the pool nearby. Perhaps admire his trophy. Revel in how it felt to act and be treated as a man, if only for a few hours.

"What lesson are you hoping to impart, Dwennon? And can you deliver it quickly?"

"The lesson I hope to impart, darling boy, is that there is no shame in losing to you. You are one of the most skilled swordsmen in the kingdom."

"No one else sees it that way." Allard finally got his chest plate off. He threw it and it clanged against his other armor.

"And they never will unless you show it to them." The wizard knew that the time was nearing when Allard would have to accept who he was, and begin the long hard road of forcing others to accept him as well. But it seemed they were not quite there yet.

So Dwennon continued to accompany Allard on his "diplomatic trips", and he watched with pride as the boy grew in confidence and skill.

As much pride as Dwennon took in Allard, he felt an equal amount of horror when he looked to Braxton, the future king. Braxton was cruel, petty, and capricious. He showed little concern for his future subjects and delighted in the potential bloodshed of war, as long as he did not have to take on any risk himself. Allard had invited Braxton to accompany himself and Dwennon on one of their visits to the front, but Braxton had grown suspicious and accused Allard of plotting to have him assassinated and threatened to have his fingernails pulled from his traitor hands. Then when Allard returned, he whined that Allard had failed to bring him a present. This was the boy who would be king.

Late one afternoon, they were studying moral philosophy in Dwennon's tower. Allard was having trouble wrapping his mind around the material. His eyes kept drifting to the window. And every time they did, Dwennon would whack him on the head with a long staff.

They were both in foul moods. It was late August. The afternoon seemed to stretch on forever. Dwennon's tower was hot and stuffy. And Allard's father was dying.

So when Allard again failed to understand what Dwennon was teaching him and was once again caught staring out the window, he lost his temper, which was actually quite rare for the young prince.

"What does any of this matter?" he cried. "What is the point of all this?" He slammed the book closed.

"To prepare you," Dwennon said.

"For what? There is no great future waiting for me. I ought to enjoy the time I have left."

"And what does that mean?"

"My father or my brother will marry me off to some king to solidify an alliance and I shall be queen of some country that will never be my home," Allard said. All of this was bad enough, that he would be forced to live far away from his heart in the beautiful kingdom he had called home all his life, but even the loss of his home was not the greatest horror he faced. "I shall be forced to live as something I am not. They'll stop me cutting my hair. Force me to wear a dress. Expect me to take up needlepoint and butterfly collecting and—and smiling. So I should enjoy the little time I have left. Enjoy the freedom to live as I truly am for a bit longer. Not waste it sitting in a stuffy room reading dusty books."

"What if you could live as you truly are forever?"

Allard snorted. "It will never happen."

"What if it could?" Dwennon asked.

"Then I would ask what it has to do with all these books."

"A king should be well rounded and well learned."

14

"I'm not going to be king," Allard said.

"And why not darling boy? You are your father's eldest son, are you not?" Dwennon said.

"You know that's not how it works. Braxton will be king. That is the law. It's what Father wants."

"I teach you all this, so that we might persuade him," Dwennon said.

Allard hesitated. It seemed too much to hope, but he wished it so. All great endeavors began with this feeling. One never did anything great without having the audacity to believe things could be better than they were.

"Do you really think he could be persuaded?"

Dwennon nodded. "I do."

Allard allowed himself a bemused smile. Then he opened his book back up. "Then I suppose we'd better get to work."

For the next few days they discussed their strategy to approach Allard's father with their proposal.

Allard had his doubts about whether any strategy would work. His father had informed him that he only called Allard by his chosen name out of deference to his mother. On the few occasions Allard had persuaded his father to take him on one of his hunting trips, the king cut the hunt short. His father seemed annoyed when he hunted well and even more annoyed when he hunted poorly, perhaps sensing that Allard was doing it deliberately. He'd never been able to determine what he could give his father that would please him. But Dwennon was very clever. And he knew people. If he said Allard's father could be persuaded, then Allard trusted him that it would work.

Eventually, they had prepared all they could. There was nothing to do, but try.

The king sat on the throne, listening to the petitions of his subjects. As always, Allard sat by the king's side and made notes on the needs of the subjects. He sat somewhat sideways in his chair, to better keep his ear pointed toward whoever was speaking so he wouldn't miss anything important in the echoing great chamber. Braxton grew bored and murmured cruel commentary to one of his advisors, who was forced to look sufficiently amused so as to not provoke Braxton's ire, but not so amused that the king grew angry at his disrespect.

Once all the petitions had been made, the king gestured for his servant to prepare his wheelchair. But then Allard stood and climbed down off the dais and knelt before the king. Dwennon joined him.

"Your majesty. I would like to petition the court," Allard said.

Braxton snorted at this.

The king gestured for Dwennon and Allard to rise. "Yes child. Speak."

Allard took a deep steadying breath. No matter what happened, things were going to be different after this. He looked his father in the eye. "I ask that you recognize me as your firstborn son and name me heir to the throne."

Braxton cackled, clapping his hands together in delight. Oh, this was most diverting.

King Cederic did not look pleased by this request, but Allard did not wilt under the power of his gaze. "Braxton is my first born son. My only son," the king said.

"Forgive me, sire, but I disagree. Born a girl I might have been, but surely you cannot look upon me now and see a daughter. I am your son and rightful heir," Allard said.

The king's advisors exploded into a flurry of whispers. Then one advisor stepped forward.

"Surely the princess is not suggesting—"

"The prince," Dwennon interrupted, "suggests nothing. He states it baldly. He should be king."

Cederic slowly shook his head, but he still hadn't said no. Not yet.

Dwennon continued quickly, hoping to finish the proposal before they were thrown from the castle or much worse. "It is customary for kings to complete great deeds before they are crowned. Is it not? Sire, before you were crowned, you slayed the ancient and terrible sea beast of Tarlborrah. So, what if you were to allow young Allard to complete such a feat? Prove himself worthy of being your heir?"

The king appeared to genuinely consider this. "And what feat do you suggest?"

Dwennon already had several feats in mind that were impressive, but well

16

within Allard's skills. "The wolf of Folsom Woods. It has stalked the folk of the nearby village for decades and none have been able to slay it." The wolf was said to be forty feet tall with an outsized appetite to match, but Dwennon knew Allard could defeat it.

The king seemed unmoved.

Dwennon next suggested the serpent of Halspard Lake or the trolls in the mountains. But the king rejected each of these suggestions.

Allard could feel his chance to be king, to be his father's son, slipping through his fingers.

"Balsinew," Allard said.

The king, Braxton, Dwennon, and all the advisors stared at him.

He and Dwennon had not discussed this, but Allard knew it was right. This was what he was meant to do, though the dragon struck fear into his heart and still haunted his nightmares. It was to be his great quest. But it would mean nothing if he wasn't afraid. There was no bravery in certain victory.

His father would never be convinced by anything less.

"I shall slay Balsinew," Allard said. "The dragon who stole a mother from her children and a great queen from her nation. I will kill Balsinew and bring you his glittering eye. Then will you recognize me as your son? As your heir?"

"Father!" Braxton cried. "Surely you cannot be considering this?"

The king ignored Braxton. He looked at Allard, really looked at him, rather than the flitting gaze he usually used, as if looking at Allard too long was painful for him.

Allard felt like he had to go on this quest. He was meant to. And beyond that, he found he *wanted* to go. The simple exuberant joy of adventure almost under way, though this feeling was quickly quashed as he looked to his younger brother's face and saw the shock and fury there. Allard felt a pang of guilt, but not enough to rescind the proposal. This was his destiny.

He turned his attention back to his father, who had finally come to a decision.

Cederic slowly nodded. "Yes. Kill that monster. And the throne is yours."

Allard nodded. "Thank you." He left the throne room before his father could change his mind. He had much to do before his quest began.

Dwennon lingered for a moment. "Thank you… sire."

The king nodded. "Send Allard to my chambers. I would have words."

Dwennon nodded and as he left the throne room he closed the door quickly behind him to muffle the sound of Braxton screaming.

3

Chapter 3

Dwennon found the prince in his room, packing.

"That was not what we discussed," Dwennon said.

"What we discussed wasn't working," Allard answered. He moved swiftly about the room, packing his compass and cartography tools in his bag. "This is what I'm meant to do, Dwennon. I'm certain of it."

Dwennon sat down heavily on the prince's bed. "Unfortunately, I'm certain as well, but it doesn't mean I have to like it. Balsinew is dangerous."

Allard moved on to packing clothes. "Most dragons are." He held up two coats for Dwennon to choose between, one dyed green leather, very sturdy, and the other plain brown leather.

Dwennon pointed to the old brown one. It would help Allard blend in. "And the road to reach him isn't so pleasant either."

Allard stuck a dagger in his boot. "I've heard parts of the journey are quite beautiful."

"Yes. It's all quite lovely until you reach the Tunnel of Interminable Suffering," Dwennon said, determined to be a pessimist. He was terrified for his young charge.

"That's funny, I had heard it was quite nice this time of year," Allard said. He hooked his sword and scabbard to his belt.

"Well you've certainly chosen a fine time to develop a sense of humor!" Dwennon cried.

Allard finally looked up from his preparations and saw the wizard's eyes full with tears. The prince rushed forward and wrapped Dwennon in a fierce hug.

"I will be alright," Allard said. "This is what is supposed to happen. I feel it. I'll kill the dragon that killed my mother. And I shall be king."

Dwennon nodded and pulled himself together. He wasn't quite finished helping the young prince. "I have some things for you," he said. He dug around in the pockets of his cloak and withdrew a cordial bottle filled with a faintly glowing blue liquid, it hung on a leather cord, the first of his gifts to the young prince. "Water of the Cave-mers," Dwennon said. "It allows you to see in the darkness. You'll need it. The Tunnel of Interminable Suffering is only nice in the winter."

Allard hung the cordial around his neck.

Next, Dwennon pulled from his pocket a spool of iridescent white thread.

"Dwennon, I think the opportunities for needlepoint on this journey will be limited," the prince said.

"Musn't make too many jokes in one sitting, sire," Dwennon said, "humor is a muscle you're just now beginning to use, we don't want to strain it." He unspooled a length of thread and stretched it up to the light. It split the sun shining through the window into a rainbow. "Unicorn hair. Amazing healing properties and perfect for stitching wounds."

Allard took the thread and placed it in his leather saddlebag.

Finally the wizard produced a simple silver ring with a large beaten stone inlaid. Though the stone was unpolished, it still caught the light and glittered every color imaginable and quite a few that weren't. "Do you know what this is?"

Allard shook his head.

"It belonged to Van Thomas the Menagerie. It will allow you to turn into any creature you choose. But only once." He handed the ring to Allard.

"So I can only be a lion once?" Allard rather liked the idea of being a lion, but if he could only do it once, he would save it for an emergency.

"Well you are welcome to try, but lion has almost certainly already been used. This thing has been circulating for centuries."

"So you can only choose each of the animals once...ever? In the entire history of the ring?" Allard turned the ring over, watching it glint in the light. They had not mentioned that in the stories of Van Thomas, though now that he thought of it, he never did turn into the same animal twice in all those adventures.

"Is that not what I just said?"

"But I don't know what's been used."

"You're clever. You'll figure something out," Dwenon said, waving his hand.

Allard smiled at this. It was what Dwennon always said when he grew tired of answering Allard's questions. Though Dwennon always did end up answering his questions eventually. He simply couldn't stand himself. He was a natural teacher.

"The key is to hold the idea of the creature in your mind, really concentrate, and speak the name of the creature you wish to become aloud. And you must be very careful," Dwennon's voice grew thick.

Allard slipped the ring on his hand. "Thank you. For this. For everything. I'll not let you down."

The wizard swiped at a tear under his dark spectacles. "You never could, my boy."

As Allard gathered his things and prepared to depart, Dwennon jolted and yelled "wait!"

Allard paused and turned back around.

"Your father asked that you come see him. Before you leave."

Allard nodded. He walked down the hallway to his father's chambers. The heels of his boots clicked and echoed off the great stone walls. He felt impossibly small, as he always did when on his way to see his father.

He knocked on the wooden door with the gold inlay depicting a forest hunting scene.

"Come in!" his father called.

Allard took a deep breath and entered.

The king sat in his wheelchair. His old sword laid across his lap, he ran a cloth over it, polishing it until the black blade glinted in the candle light. "Come sit by me a moment," the king said.

Allard walked to him and knelt in front of him.

"You know the way?" his father asked gruffly.

"Yes."

His father continued as if Allard hadn't answered. "Through Prism Valley. You'll want to wait until the evening."

"Yes," Allard said.

"Then the Upside Down Lake. Don't dally. Just because it's pretty doesn't mean it can't be dangerous." His father's voice grew more rough the longer he spoke.

"Yes sire."

"Then the tunnel."

"Yes."

"You could go around," his father said. Or maybe he was asking.

Allard shook his head. "No. I can't."

A single tear rolled down his father's cheek. He stared straight ahead. "You come back." His voice shook with vehemence.

"Yes, Father."

His father reached out and took Allard's hand. He drew it to his mouth and held it to his lips, squeezing it perhaps a bit too hard. Finally he removed Allard's hand from his lips and placed it on the hilt of his sword. "Take this."

Allard's breath hitched in his throat. Forged from the metal of a fallen star, the sword had been passed down for generations. It had been created for the first of their line, the first to be born with rain falling and the sun shining at the same time. His grandfather had led their kingdom to victory in wars against many enemies with it. His father had slain the seabeast with it. And it had tasted Balsinew's blood before. Allard curled his fingers around the hilt.

His father patted his hand, desperately as if it was all that was keeping him together. "May it serve you well and strike true," the king said. His voice had a watery quality.

Allard knew his father would not want him to see his tears and so, to preserve the king's dignity, he kept his eyes cast downward as he gave his father a hug. Then he rose and swapped out his sword for his father's in his scabbard.

"Thank you, Father."

Allard closed the door to his father's chamber. He had one last stop to make before he departed.

He knocked on the door to his brother's room.

"Go away, I said I didn't want any!" Braxton screamed.

"Braxton. It's me," Allard said.

There was a loud crash, some stomping footsteps and then Braxton ripped open the door. "What do you want?"

He'd been crying. His pale skin and dark eyes made the redness particularly obvious. His eyelashes had that sodden quality only ever caused by crying and his voice was choked with snot.

"Can I come in?"

Braxton stood back and let Allard in. "Sizing it up for when you steal it?" Braxton asked as he gestured wildly around the room. It was the second largest room in the castle after their father's.

"I don't want to steal your room."

"No. Just my throne," Braxton sneered.

Allard sat down on the edge of Braxton's bed and beckoned for his brother to join him. Braxton sat down.

"It doesn't have to be this way. You could come with me. We could defeat Balsinew together. Rule *together*." Allard didn't want to steal away what Braxton felt was his, but he was realistic enough to know that Braxton could not be allowed to rule on his own. But Braxton was smart, ruling together, they could be great.

For a moment, just one moment, Allard allowed himself to believe Braxton might say yes. That they could be true brothers.

And maybe Braxton did consider it, for a moment. But then he saw the hilt of their father's sword sticking out of Allard's scabbard and Allard saw cold hatred turn Braxton's eyes flat and dull.

"He's going to kill you," Braxton hissed. "He's going to kill you and I'll be glad."

Allard nodded. It was time to go.

He rose and left Braxton's room as his brother chanted, "He's going to kill you and I'll be glad. He's going to kill you and I'll be glad." Braxton's words echoed off the great stone walls as Allard walked back up the hallway and toward the great staircase. "He's going to kill you and I'll be glad."

The words continued to echo in Allard's head as he saddled his beautiful black horse, Ondine. But once he passed the castle gates, he allowed himself to think of them no more. He was on a quest.

4

Chapter 4

Allard rode hard the first day. Balsinew's lair was at least a week's ride away and that was if he ran into no problems. But he'd read enough books about great quests to know that he was going to run into at least a few problems.

Allard was not the only one riding hard. Unbeknownst to Allard, after destroying his room in a fit of rage, Braxton had summoned one of his advisors and told him to find the fastest rider he could, to go hire the kind of men who would do any number of despicable things for money.

After a day and a half of riding, Allard arrived at the edge of the Prism Valley. Bows of colored light shot jubilantly into the sky. He'd reached the valley at high noon, when the valley was at its most stunning. And dangerous.

The valley was composed of gigantic prismatic crystal structures that were as hypnotic as they were confusing. It was easy to step off a ledge into a chasm that looked like it was only two feet below but was, in fact, hundreds of feet deep, simply a trick of the light.

Allard sat down at the crest of the valley. He would wait until early evening, when the light was more diluted, before he started his trek. It should only take a few hours to navigate, and he could make camp for the night on the other side.

Allard pulled out the pair of darkened spectacles Dwennon had gifted him several years before, very similar to the ones the wizard himself wore at all times. Allard had been dubious of their usefulness, but had to admit that they had come in handy a time of two. He watched the light in the valley dance and shift as the sun traveled across the sky.

While he waited, he decided to practice with the ring. He supposed most of the good animals were taken. He murmured to himself as he mulled over what animal he should try first. How nice it would be to just be able to turn into a "bear." He accidentally said the word aloud. A burst of light shot out of the ring and suddenly Allard was nine feet tall with gigantic paws. He let out a giant roar, but was too surprised to concentrate properly, and thus immediately turned back into a human.

He cursed himself a fool. Bear had still been available and he'd wasted it. He tried the bear again, just to be certain it was truly gone, but the ring did nothing. Allard remained human. He spent the next couple of hours turning into various bugs and rodents to get used to holding the idea of the animal in his mind. He could only manage it for a few minutes before the animal's senses overwhelmed him, and he once again shifted back into a human. Once, he named a very obscure rodent from a realm on the other side of the world and found it had already been taken. He wondered about the ring's previous owners and what circumstance had led them to that particular animal. Or had they just been practicing as well?

Finally, he deemed it safe to enter the valley, which quickly turned into a narrow, labyrinthian canyon. He would have to lead his horse so he could feel in front of him and make sure the ground was solid. He'd packed a bag of sand and he now poked a hole in it with his dagger. A stream of sand ran from the hole to indicate what route he had taken. There was very little wind in the valley so the sand wouldn't be disturbed, and it would show him a safe route on his return journey. Wistfully, Allard wished he had the time to map the valley properly. He shook his head. Another time.

Slowly, through the Prism Valley they traveled. The canyon floor was littered with the bodies of broken-necked birds who had gotten confused and flown into the large crystal structures that loomed overhead. Every once in a while, his horse balked, tossing her head and Allard would have to gently coax her forward, show her that it was safe. The light in the valley grew deeper and more saturated as the sun began to set, which took hours this time of year.

The canyon branched off, and he would have to choose a route and pray it was right. Several times he had to double back and choose a different path as one led to a sudden drop off or dead end.

Allard and Ondine had just squeezed through a particularly narrow section when a bird thunked into one of the crystalline structures and dropped onto his horse's back.

Ondine panicked and reared up. Her hooves struck some of the crystal over their heads and chunks of it rained down on Allard, embedding in his hair and covering his face in little nicks.

Allard tightened his grip on the reins and tried to calm his horse.

The bird spasmed and tangled in Ondine's mane. She started to buck, hopping up and down, kicking out with her powerful hind legs. She broke off a chunk of crystal, and then, on the next kick, dragged her flank across the edge and tore a deep jagged gash in her flesh. If he didn't get her calmed down, she was really going to hurt herself.

"Shhhhhh, darling, it's alright," Allard soothed, but Ondine tossed her head and backed up. Allard held firm. He managed to get the dying bird untangled from her mane. He cast it aside. "It's okay. It was just a bird. It's okay. Shhhhhhhh."

Eventually he calmed her down enough that he was able to look at the gouge in her flank. The sand from the bag pooled at their feet."Okay, my darling. I'm going to sew this up for you. Alright? It'll feel better in just a moment."

Allard dug around in his bag and retrieved the unicorn hair thread. For the first time, he was glad that his parents had forced him to learn to sew.

He threaded the needle. "I'm sorry darling. This is going to hurt. I'll try to be quick."He petted her softly for a moment before stitching the torn flesh back together. Ondine whinnied in pain, but she held still.

Soon, he was done. And by the time he tied off the last stitch, the first stitch was nearly healed. He wrapped his arms around her neck and then rubbed her nose affectionately. "Well. That's all squared away isn't it?"

So great was his relief at being able to move forward again, Allard forgot to feel where he was going. The ground before him, which seemed so solid, was not actually there, was nothing more than a trick of the light.

He was too far gone to regain his balance. He was already over the edge and would have dropped to the chasm floor a hundred feet below, except that he still held Ondine's reins. He grabbed at them desperately before they could slide from his hands. He managed to catch hold and stop himself from plunging to his death. He looked down once, and only once, to watch the darkened glasses from Dwennon fall for a long time before hitting the ground. The chasm was deep and lined with jagged crystals jutting from the sides. And he'd just as soon not be reminded of what might await him.

Ondine reared up again and Allard almost lost his grip, but he grimly held on, the leather of the reins digging into his hands. "Shhhhh," he said, the uneven broken quality of his voice betraying his fear. "I-it's okay Ondine. Shhhhh."

Ondine struck at the ground a few times with her hooves.

"Shhhh darling. Shhh." Allard readjusted his grip on the reins."Back up Ondine. Back back back." He clicked at her with his mouth. "Back up darling."

The horse began to calm. She backed up slowly, very slowly, but finally, she backed up far enough that Allard was able to get his arms back on the ledge. But he did not let go of the reins until he was safely back on solid ground.

He flopped onto his back, breathing hard. He watched as the gigantic crystals caught the first stars breaking through the sky. He had to get out of here before dark.

Before moving forward he double, triple, quadruple checked to make sure the ground was solid. It made for slow going, but they were able to exit the Prism Valley without further incident and soon made camp on the other side.

Allard would have preferred an area less open and exposed, but there was nothing but gentle, rolling hills for miles. He led Ondine down to a flat area below the hilltop where he would sleep. He drove a stake into the ground and tied her lead rope to it, satisfied that she would have plenty to eat as there was fine green grass all around her, then climbed the hill again and built a small fire. He eschewed a tent, preferring to sleep on his side so he could watch the

Prism Valley reflect and refract the stars into infinity.

In the small hours of the morning, before the sun started to rise, Allard awoke to the sound of quiet footsteps whispering across the grass. Allard only had enough time to throw aside his blanket, stand, and draw his sword, before the men were upon him: six of them, a band of highwaymen or bandits.

The bandits drew in a tight circle around Allard. When one tried to grab him, he scared them back with his sword, and then another tried to take him from behind and he whirled to stop them. He put up quite a fight for a long time, but they could afford to be patient; they wore him down, attacking in rotating groups, forcing Allard to defend himself.

Strike and parry. Strike and parry. Eventually he grew so tired he let his body move on its own, reacting with pure instinct. This lent a sharpness to his fighting for a time, but was unsustainable.

"You don't have much quit, I'll give ya that," one of the men said. He cackled, Allard bashed him in the chest, cutting off his laughter and sending him sprawling to the ground. The bandit had significantly fewer observations after that.

Allard was sure there was more talk. He could almost comprehend what the bandits were saying, but he had to focus all his energy on defeating them, and their voices faded to a distant drone as Allard grew more and more tired.

The fight stretched on as the sun rose and shards of pink and orange light glared at them from the valley. If Allard had to fight any of them one on one, even two or three on one, he would have easily defeated them. But the bandits weren't interested in honor or a fair fight— they were interested in taking Allard down.

They succeeded. Though not before he stuck one in the gut with his sword. It wouldn't kill him, but it certainly wasn't pleasant either.

The bandits piled on top of Allard. He squirmed and writhed, trying to get out from under them, but they held him down. They peeled themselves off the pile one at a time, keeping Allard pinned before grabbing him under the arms and dragging him back to his feet.

They looked to the ostensible leader of the group, a man with an eyepatch embroidered with golden thread. "This the one?" one of the bandits, an unfortunate skinny fellow with wooden teeth, asked.

Eyepatch squinted his good eye and gave Allard a serious once over. "Blonde hair, green eyes, real pretty, oh aye, that's the one."

"Who sent you?" Allard demanded.

Eyepatch smirked. "Don't be askin' questions ye already know the answers to."

Of course, Allard's brother sent them. Not content to simply leave his fate up to chance, Braxton had decided to send these highwaymen to capture Allard and make sure he didn't complete his quest.

If Allard could get the ring to work then he might be able to escape. But he couldn't just speak the names of five or ten animals and pray it worked. The bandits would notice something was afoot. He had to be clever, the way Dwennon had taught him.

"And what might your name bee?" Allard asked. Unfortunately he didn't turn into a bee and fly away.

"Never mind all that," Eyepatch grunted. "You don't need to know."

"When there's a fox in the henhouse I like to know as much as I can," Allard said.

"Get used to disappointment," Eyepatch said. He jerked his head and the goons holding Allard's arms started to drag him away.

Allard dug in his heels. "Let's address the elephant in the room," he said, feeling faintly ridiculous but adhering to the course of action he'd chosen. He was too tired to try and fight more. In fact, if the goons hadn't been holding him up, he'd be on his knees, unable to stand or lift his arms. The ring was his only hope.. "My brother is a snake. He's as likely to feed you to the wolves as he is to actually pay you. Sorry to let the cat out of the bag, but he's a one trick pony."

"What're you doing?" Eyepatch asked.

"He'll weasel out of any agreement you had. Don't be pig-headed, you're a sitting duck," Allard said.

"Shut him up," Eyepatch said.

"Now as much as I'd like to let sleeping dogs lie—" Allard began.

"Shut him up!" Eyepatch yelled.

Skinny tried to clamp his grimy hand over Allard's mouth but he shook him loose.

"—but if anything happens to me, you'll be the scapegoat." Allard jerked his head away as Skinny tried to cover his mouth again. " I'm not…" he squeezed his eyes shut, last chance, "Lion."

Allard's body quickly grew too heavy to hold up, and his captors let him drop down to all fours as his hands turned to large paws and his hair turned into a proud golden mane. He roared and slashed at the men closest to him with his claws.

A man with a bow slung across his back fumbled to pull it over his head. Allard pounced on top of him and snapped it. The man screamed and tried to squirm out from under Allard. Allard clawed at the man's shoulder.

Allard felt a horrible pain in his back, he turned to look and saw that one of the men had stabbed him with his own abandoned sword.

Allard roared and bit down on his assailant's leg. The assailant screamed and pounded his fists on Allard's head but he did not let go.

The men tried to fight back, but they could not defeat the mighty lion. Allard hurt them enough that they couldn't follow him, but he left them alive.

Once he'd dropped his final assailant, Allard let the lion slip from his mind and he turned back into a man. He grabbed his sword and a few of his things, keeping careful watch that none of the men recovered enough to stop him.

Allard made his way down the hillside to his horse on trembling legs. He was worn to the bone, and while the stab wound from his sword wasn't deep, it was still painful. When he finally reached Ondine, he found he didn't have the strength to stand, let alone hoist himself up. He buried his face in the grass and laughed bitterly to himself, wondering what he was going to do if those men got back up and he was still there, marvelling at the stupidity of the situation he'd found himself in.

Ondine knelt down beside him, getting as low as she could. He stared at her for a moment, hardly believing. But she remained in place, waiting for him.

With a groan, he sat up. He threw one of his legs over Ondine's back and slowly, laboriously, pulled himself into the saddle. Once he was settled,

Ondine stood back up, careful not to unseat her passenger. Allard wrapped his arms tightly around her and hugged her.

"Thank you darl—" Allard passed out without finishing the last word, his arm's still wrapped around Ondine's neck.

Ondine started walking. She kept a good pace but was very careful not to accidentally dump Allard onto the ground. They passed small forests, rivers, and villages. All the while, Allard slept.

5

Chapter 5

It was midday before Allard awoke to Ondine tossing her head and striking at the ground.

They had reached the Upside Down Lake. She really was the most magnificent horse.

Allard had read books about the lake, had seen illustrations. But they in no way prepared him to see it in person: a blue lake with water clear as glass, floating in the air. Fish swam with their bellies to the sky. Pondweeds grew down toward the surface.

Allard nudged Ondine forward, and grudgingly, she moved. Her hooves kicked up little puffs of dust as she walked across the dry lake bed. Allard tilted his head back and watched as the fish darted about in upside down schools. He reached up and gently pushed a lilypad with the very tips of his fingers and sent it drifting away.

As he rode further, the lake grew deeper and the ground grew darker. He could see the shapes of fish and merpeople silhouetted as the sun shone through the water. They traveled deeper still.

He would have liked to have stayed there, watching the busy lake in action, but giant creatures cast long shadows as they swam above him, and there was little to keep them from breaching the surface and eating him up if they grew hungry. His father had been right. This place was dangerous. Allard needed to move along. He clicked his tongue and Ondine was only too happy to kick into a gallup and get to the other side of the Upside Down Lake.

Soon the lakebed in front of them began to lighten; as they reached the shallows, the surface of the lake grew lower and lower until Allard had to slump over Ondine's neck to keep his head out of the water. Ondine stretched her neck up and drank deeply from the lake. Once she'd drunk her fill, she stepped out from under the lake drenching Allard as she scrambled up the steep bank.

Allard rode for two days, watching the landscape change as the Morphing Mountain, through which the Tunnel of Interminable Suffering ran, grew larger. Soon he was close enough to see the rocks crashing and falling as ledges and cliffs rose and collapsed. Nothing could grow there. The mountain was just brutal slate grey rock.

The face of the Morphing Mountain was always changing. It was impossible to climb. It would take too long to detour around it. Allard had no choice but to pass through. As he got closer to the mountain, he found it next to impossible to sleep because of the distant rumbling of the mountain shifting in its slumber.

He didn't expect to find anyone living so close to the entrance of the tunnel, but there was a tidy little cottage up ahead, ringed with sunflowers. Chickens bustled about, clucking at each other indignantly. A cow serenely munched on a mouthful of grass. Bees buzzed around a roughly-hewn hive. In front of the cottage was an old woman with long flowing grey hair, on her hands and knees, weeding a garden. All this stood not 30 yards from the mouth of the Tunnel of Interminable Suffering. Allard, who had expected the entrance to the Tunnel to be a desolate, lifeless place, could hardly believe it.

As he got closer to the Morphing Mountain, the sound grew. The grinding and crashing were near unbearable, though Allard would be the first to admit he had a low threshold for loud noises. Ever since Balsinew had nearly deafened him as a child, harsh noises pained him greatly.

But the great cacophony of the ever-shifting mountain was silent. Allard could hear birds singing. He could hear his own breathing. All was quiet within the area surrounding the old woman's home.

Allard dismounted from Ondine and walked toward the woman, slowly so as to not startle her. The woman pulled at a particularly large weed, but it would not free from the ground. She laboriously climbed to her feet and wrapped her hands around the weed's stalk and gave it a great yank, but it still wouldn't come loose. She still hadn't noticed Allard.

"Hello!" he called. "May I help?"

The old woman looked up and smiled. Her eyes danced with good cheer and the corners of her eyes crinkled.

"Oh aye, ye might have better luck than me," the woman said.

She stood back, swiping her hair out of her eyes with the back of her hand so as not to get dirt on her face, and smudging her forehead with dark soil anyway. Allard stepped forward and pulled on the weed's stalk. At first it didn't want to move for him either, but eventually, he felt the tell-tale crumble that meant the roots were about to give. The weed came free. He tossed it aside.

"You pull weeds quite well for someone dressed so fine," the woman said.

Allard looked down in surprise. He'd chosen his most nondescript clothing for the journey. "I had a good teacher," Allard said, "he thought it was important I know how it felt to put in an honest day's work. If I might ask, what gave me away?"

The woman laughed, "Oh, it isn't anything obvious. But I know where to look." She pointed to his boots which were deep oxblood leather. Then she pointed to the thin gold chain hung around his neck with a small gold medal that bore his mother's likeness. His father and brother both wore identical ones. Finally she gestured to Ondine and the armor, which was old but expensive, strapped to the back of the saddle. "So. Did this very good teacher of yours teach you to milk cows?"

Allard smiled. "He did."

"Well if you wouldn't mind milking Esperanza over there, I'll get started on our dinner." And with that she walked back toward the cottage.

Well. It would appear he'd been invited to dinner. Allard hadn't planned to enter the tunnel until morning anyway, so he was glad to stay and have a meal. Allard looked around for a moment, not sure where she kept the—

"Bucket's over there," she pointed to her right without breaking stride or turning around. "Stool's over there." She pointed to her left.

After he milked the cow, he peeked in the chicken coop and saw the eggs hadn't been collected yet. So he gathered them. Then he noticed that there was a broken section on her fence, so he went inside, briefly, to ask the woman where she kept her tools, and fixed the fence. Then he got to thinking that the front step was a bit wobbly and it wouldn't do for the old woman to take a tumble out here all alone with no one to help her. So he fixed that as well.

As the sun began to set, the old woman stuck her head out the door. "Before you decide to build me a winter estate, you'd better come in! Dinner is almost ready."

Allard swiped the sweat from his forehead with the back of his arm and stretched to crack his back as he walked into the cottage, where he was overwhelmed by the smell of cooking food. For the last week he'd been subsisting on dried meat and tough bread that got tougher every day.

The old woman had at least eight different things cooking. There was a pot of pleasantly bubbling bright orange carrot soup. She'd placed a couple of potatoes amongst the coals under the hob, and their jackets were deliciously blackened. There were lamb chops crusted with rosemary and garlic flowers, a loaf of cracked crust bread, a bowl of wild greens and berries. A blackberry pie cooled on the windowsill.

"It's been quite some time since I've had company. I guess I'm just a little excited," she said.

Allard murmured, "You do too much, Old Mother."

She smiled at the old-fashioned affectation. Old Mother. So formal. "I think I do just enough," she said, "especially when I'm dining with nobility."

It was clear the boy was a noble, not just some rich merchant's son. She thought he might be an earl, perhaps even a duke. He had those stiff manners, the old but expensive armor, that beautiful horse. She wondered what had brought him so far from home.

"My teacher will be very disappointed that I didn't blend in better."

"Mm. Lost cause, I'm afraid. You're quite a striking young man. Doomed to stick out. But that will serve you well." The old woman poked at the potatoes with a long fork. Not quite done. "So. Marquis? Earl?"

The young man forced a chuckle. "Nothing so grand. Just a lord. And a minor one at that. One who longs for adventure and does not like to stand on ceremony."

"Good. Nor do I," the old woman said.

"Though I must apologize Old Mother, I never asked for your name."

The old woman smiled a private smile. The boy had called her Old Mother again; despite his claims that he didn't like to stand on ceremony she'd never met someone so unfailingly polite, it was rather endearing. She stood up slowly, grumbling good-naturedly about her cracking joints. "My name is Wendla. And what shall I call you?"

"Allard."

Wendla whistled softly. "After the Green, I'd imagine. Quite a name to live up to."

Allard nodded gravely. "I'm doing my best."

Wendla stirred the soup, tasted it, and deemed it ready. She pulled two wooden bowls from the cupboard and instructed Allard to get the potatoes out of the fire. Soon enough, the entire feast was laid out before them. "So, you're going through the tunnel."

"Yes."

"And you wish to slay the dragon? On the other side?"

"Yes."

"What are you chasing? Glory? Fame?"

Allard appeared to seriously consider the question before he shook his head slowly. "No. Not fame. Not glory."

"Then what?"

Even if Allard had been able to tell her the whole story he doubted he would have been able to explain it. He had a mind for maps. He had a mind for strategy. He could fight and he could dance. But he couldn't speak on matters of the heart. He always ended up explaining himself rather poorly. Only Dwennon had much chance of prying anything out of him. And Wendla was a stranger.

He chose the more obvious answer, so he didn't have to try and explain fathers and sons and forbidden toy soldiers. "My mother. She was taken when I was very young. I'm going to avenge her. Make sure Balsinew never breaks apart another family. Then the kingdom will no longer have to live in fear."

"I'm sorry to hear about your mother."

"She was the bravest person I ever knew," Allard said. "And funny. My father is quite...stiff. Formal. She was the only one who could get him to smile. Only times I ever heard him laugh was after something she said. Oh yes, sometimes she'd call herself his jester, and he'd get all puffed up at the impropriety of it, but eventually he would laugh, he'd always laugh, in the end."

The young man smiled, lost in memory for a moment. Wendla studied him closer. She had a theory on who he really was. She was almost sure. And this made her feel guilty, as he clearly did not want to be identified, and so she purposefully kept her mind from putting the pieces fully together.

They ate quietly for a bit, until Allard broke the silence. "Old M-Wendla. Why do you live so close to the tunnel?"

"Like my father before me and my daughter will after me, I live here to warn off people like you. Try and convince you not to go through. My husband lives on the other side of the tunnel, and does the same. We see each other only a few times each year. For centuries, my family has done our best to protect those that would go through the tunnel. So I beg you—go around, Allard. It may take longer, but it's better than dying under that mountain."

Allard had his jaw set in a way that made Wendla very worried. "I can't go around," Allard said. "It'll be too late."

She cocked an eyebrow at him. "Too late? Are you expecting someone else to slay the dragon before you do? Are you worried Balsinew is going to die of old age before you get there?"

"My father is dying. I have to-I have to bring him Balsinew's eye before-he has to know that I-" Allard took a steadying breath, "he has to know that I did it. That I slayed the dragon."

After sharing much more than he'd intended (how did she do that?), Allard concentrated very hard on his bowl of soup.

Wendla was greatly saddened. She liked Allard and there would be no swaying him. There rarely was. The kind of person who would consider entering a place as dangerous as the The Tunnel of Interminable Suffering was unlikely to be persuaded by the words of an old woman. So she did what she could. She gave these travelers a good meal, a few words of advice, and sent them off, sent them to their death. "So you are quite decided," Wendla said.

Allard sagged with relief that the discussion seemed to be coming to a close. "Yes. Quite decided."

"Then I shall not scratch at you and we can enjoy our evening."

They spent the rest of the meal in pleasant conversation. Wendla agreed to watch Ondine, as Allard would not be able to take her into the tunnel. Allard told her amusing stories about his teacher Dwennon. And once they'd finished eating, Wendla asked to see some of Allard's maps.

Allard eagerly pulled them from his bag. He showed her where he had added the Prism Valley and the Upside Down Lake. He told her of his adventures, pointing out their locations on his beautifully-illustrated maps. He jumped from marvels great to small: the view from under Upside Down Lake to a flock of sheep dotting a grassy hill. The Sunset Waterfalls of the southern tip of the realm. A small creek that ran behind a farmer's house. He was in the midst of describing the view from a particular bluff that overlooked a rock quarry, but a very pretty rock quarry, when Wendla's brain refused to continue pretending she didn't know who he was.

He talked about the kingdom like a lover. Like she was *his*. "You really love this place don't you?" Wendla asked.

Allard flashed his eyes up at her. "I'd walk every mile and know every inch, if I could." He fondly smoothed out a corner of the map that threatened to curl up. He showed her a few more maps, and then she invited him to sit outside under the stars.

6

Chapter 6

Wendla had a couple chairs set up outside. Sometimes, taking those planning to go through the tunnel outside, and showing them the stars, was enough to convince them it wasn't worth it to die in the dark. She knew that would be a fruitless endeavor with Allard and so she simply took her pipe out of her pocket, lit it, and enjoyed the stars.

The burning tobacco in her pipe lit her face with the faintest orange glow. "Would you like to be king? Allard?" She asked, quite casually.

She didn't have to look at him to see Allard stiffen.

He adopted a nonchalant voice. "There would have to be quite a confluence of events for that to happen. The line of succession stretches on and on before it would ever reach me."

"I think you're quite a lot closer to the throne then you let on."

Allard darted a glance at her. She only saw the white of his eye in the darkness.

"Perhaps I should not call you Allard," Wendla said.

Allard often found himself in the miserable position of having to either lie about his name and station or lie about who he *was*. There were few people on this earth with whom he could tell both truths at the same time. And when he was forced to choose, he chose to be as he truly was rather than pretending to be a girl just to please his father or the court or anyone else. He'd lied to Wendla about who he was so that he could be honest with her about the things that mattered. But those things would be quickly overshadowed now that she knew his true identity. Once they knew, it was never the same. He braced for her to say, "Perhaps I should call you Princess." They all did. In the end.

"Perhaps I should be calling you Prince Allard," Wendla said.

Allard let out a surprised huff. Wendla could see the shadow of his hand fly up to his face to wipe under his eyes.

When Allard did speak, his voice was thick, "Yes. That would be fine."

With nothing else to hide, he explained to her the full scope of his quest. How if he succeeded he would be crowned king and finally be called his father's son.

Occasionally, Wendla did have visitors and they often brought news. So, she knew a bit of Braxton, the current heir to the throne. And she thought Allard would be a much better choice. He spoke with such great care and he clearly loved the kingdom and her people. And of course she had heard the tales of the rain on a cloudless day. Everyone had.

She had to do her part to make sure Allard succeeded. Now that she knew him, she could not bear to send him off like the others.

"It is time for this old woman to go to bed. I would offer you the spare cot I have, but the grass out here will be softer and the view much better. But please, do not leave in the morning without saying goodbye." With that, Wendla rose and walked back toward her cottage.

That night, Allard slept better than he had since the quest began. Possibly better than he ever had in his life. And in the morning he arose, ready to enter the tunnel, though not before saying goodbye to the woman who had been so kind to him.

As Allard sat in the grass, sorting through his belongings, determining what he could pack on his back, Wendla exited the cottage balancing two plates of fried eggs, bacon, and strawberries, mugs of strong black tea, and a little ornate silver box.

Allard shot to his feet and took the plates and one of the mugs from her. She led him over to the little table that sat between the two chairs they'd sat in the night before. They sat down. Allard waited for her to start eating.

"Go on, tuck in," Wendla said.

She watched him eat with a sad sort of smile on her face. Then she finally ate herself, though she mostly picked at the food.

Finally, once Allard had finished eating, Wendla said, "I have something for you."

She opened the lid of the little silver box. Lying on an ancient cushion of faded blue velvet was a white dewdrop flower with a little bell shaped blossom that hung off a curved stem.

"This flower is what allows me to travel through the tunnel and visit my husband on the other side. It keeps me safe. I want you to have it."

The flowers were quite rare. This was the only one she'd ever been able to find. And if Allard died or didn't bring it back, then she might not see her love again for many years, because she could not survive a journey through the tunnel without it.

Wendla held up her finger and looked at him quite severely. "To borrow. Not to keep. This means you have to promise me that you'll survive to bring it back. Yes?"

Allard smiled. "Yes. I promise, Old Mother."

Wendla stood up and gestured for him to do the same. Then she marched over and placed her ear to his chest. Allard startled at first but then held still as she moved around. Finally she gave herself a nod and placed a finger directly over his heart.

"You keep it pinned over your heart. And you be safe." Wendla sniffed back a few tears.

Allard wrapped his arms around her. "Thank you. Thank you so much."

Soon Allard was ready. He said goodbye to Wendla; he said goodbye to Ondine, then he entered the tunnel.

7

Chapter 7

The light from outside faded very quickly. Wendla had given him a torch, but it would run out soon and Allard would be forced to rely on the water of the Cave-mers. As he walked, he compulsively checked to make sure the dewdrop flower was still pinned over his heart. The only sound beyond his footsteps was the muted rumble of the Morphing Mountain above.

Allard had been walking for an hour and had yet to suffer any fate worse than bumping his head on a stalactite. He supposed Wendla's flower must be working.

Then he heard something run past him in the darkness. He whirled around, his torch burning a white stripe across his vision as his eyes struggled to adjust, and searched for the source of the noise.

He waited a few moments then began walking again.

Again, he heard the patter of little footsteps and the rustling of clothes.

"Who's there? Show yourself," Allard commanded. He drew his sword and put his back to the wall so no one could sneak up on him.

Allard's partially-deafened ear made it difficult to gauge how close the footsteps were, though he was able to tell they were coming from the wrong direction. Whatever had slipped past him had run back toward the entrance of the tunnel. Allard was sure of it. But he could tell they were coming from deeper in the tunnel. Whoever it was, they were either very fast or there was more than one of them.

Then the sound was right on top of him, and he brandished his sword while reaching out to grab whoever or whatever it was. Allard's fingers grasped cloth and the figure, who was apparently quite small, nearly jerked over backwards.

The figure let out a scared wail. Allard lowered his torch and saw that it was a child.: a little boy of about 7 or 8. He let go of the child and crouched down. The kid tried to take off again. His eyes were wild with fear and his forehead was speckled with blood as if he had run very hard into one of the tunnel walls.

Allard gently corralled him, keeping the child from disappearing back into the tunnel and getting lost again.

"We have to go! " The boy screamed. He looked back the way he'd come and ducked down quickly, as if avoiding a predatory bird, but there was nothing there.

"How long have you been in here?" Allard asked.

The boy ignored his questions and kept darting glances all around, though the rest of his body was completely rigid, as if he was too scared to move.

Allard knelt down, moving slowly and deliberately so as not to frighten the boy further. He kept his voice soft."What's your name. Hm? Mine's Allard."

The boy responded by letting out a great scream that pierced Allard's ears and bounced in great jags down the tunnel.

Allard tried to calm the boy. "Hey. It's okay. It's alright."

"It's coming!" the boy shrieked. He pointed over Allard's shoulder.

Allard turned around, but as far as he could tell, the tunnel was empty except for the two of them. "There's nothing there. There's nothing there," Allard said in a calming rhythmic voice. "You're just scared. It's alright I'm gonna get—"

The boy's legs lifted off the ground of their own accord, as if something had picked him up by the back of his shirt and was dragging him away, except there was nothing there.

The child screamed and thrashed against his attacker. Allard reached out and caught hold of the boy's hands. He nearly succeeded in pulling the boy back down to the ground, but the invisible assailant moved with renewed vigor and nearly tore the boy out of his hands.

"Pleeeeease!" the boy screamed. "Pleeeeease don't let it get me!"

Allard still had no idea what "it" was, no idea how big it was, all he knew was that it was strong and fast.

Allard dropped his weight, pulling the boy back down close to the ground, but the invisible creature held fast. Allard saw the back of the boy's shirt ripping. He gave the boy's hand one more tremendous pull and the collar ripped. He brought the boy close. The boy locked his legs around Allard's waist and wrapped his arms around Allard's neck.

Allard swung his sword a few times but of course hit nothing but air.

"Do you see it?" Allard asked.

"To the left!" the boy said.

Allard swept his sword to the left but didn't hit anything.

"It swooped up. Behind you!" The kid said.

Allard jabbed forward and felt his sword connect with something.

"You caught its foot," the boy said. Then, he scanned the tunnel. "Coming back around. To the right."

Allard sliced through the air to his right and felt his sword jerk in his hands as he hit something substantial. He drew back and swung again. He hit the creature again.

"It's really hurt," the boy said. "Put me down."

Allard sat the boy down again. He handed the torch over to the child so he could use both hands on his sword. He hacked and slashed at the creature, not sure where to aim so as to do the most damage, missing completely a few times.

Finally the boy said, "Wait. I think it's dead. I think it—"

The boy fell over as his feet were jerked out from under him. The torch dropped out of his hand and into a puddle, plunging the tunnel into darkness. The child could no longer be his eyes and there was no time to use the water of the Cave-mers. Allard drew his sword up far over his head and plunged it straight at the ground right in front of the child's foot.

It sank into the creature. The creature released the child, and Allard drove the blade ever more deeply.

The boy scrambled backwards, getting as far from the creature as he could, cutting his hands on the rock.

Allard pulled out his blade, stabbing the creature again and again.

The child came forward a little bit, very wary, then he relaxed. He kicked the invisible creature several times."Yes. It's dead this time."

Allard tried to pull the kid away but the kid kept kicking the dead thing, tears running down his face.

8

Chapter 8

A llard picked the kid up and the boy instantly melted into him and buried his face in the crook of Allard's neck, sobbing.

"It's okay. You're safe now," Allard murmured, holding the little boy tight though he doubted the validity of his own words. Hadn't he already been wrong once?

But the creature had only gone after the child. It had ignored Allard completely, even when he had been killing it. Finally, he realized—the flower!

"I know how to keep you safe, but I'm going to have to set you down again. Alright?"

The boy nodded and Allard gently put him back on the ground. Then, Allard unpinned the flower and pinned it to the boy's shirt, right over his heart.

"This flower will keep you safe. But you have to keep it safe in return. It belongs to a friend of mine and she'll be wanting it back. Can you do that—what's your name?"

"Layne," the boy said.

"Can you do that, Layne?"

The boy nodded.

"Now. Where did you come from?"

Layne told Allard that he was from the Village Black, which was in the direction Layne was already headed. Allard promised the boy that he would get him home.

The boy picked up the torch. It was soaking wet and wouldn't light. The boy went a bit wobbly. "I'm sorry," he said. Then his voice got so small it broke Allard's heart, "I'm scared of the dark."

Allard adopted a rather grandiose voice, designed to make Layne giggle. "Be of good cheer, Layne. I've got just the thing." Then he pulled out the bottle of Water of the Cave-mers from under his shirt. It glowed faintly in the darkness. Allard uncorked the bottle and handed it to Layne. "Tiny sip."

Layne held the bottle up to his face, in the soft glow Allard could see him eyeing the liquid doubtfully. "What is it?"

"It's from deep sea merpeople. Makes it so you can see in the dark," Allard said.

Layne took a sip. "Tastes weird." He handed the bottle to Allard.

Allard took a small sip. The liquid coated his tongue like an oil, except it was sweet, unpleasantly sweet, like overripe fruit, on its way to rotting, and quite salty as well.

Allard was so focused on the taste that at first he didn't notice the change in his surroundings. He looked down at his feet and saw the slain creature, now visible. It was a large flying lizard with webbed wings and fur. Its fur was white and glowed bright as the Water of the Cave-mers took hold. Blue glowing blood coated its fur and the walls of the cave, as well as the boy and Allard himself. Without the flower, he could now feel the blood drying to a crust on his face.

Allard looked down the tunnel and was surprised to find it had an absolute riot of color, when before it had just been plain rock. Now, every surface was positively caked with obscenely bright fungi and lichen.

"Does anything look different?" Allard asked. "Now that you're wearing the flower?"

Rather than looking around, the boy instead felt along the wall. "All the soft stuff is gone. It was always too dark for me to see but the walls were soft. Squishy."

Allard reached out and touched the wall. Indeed it was. At least he'd be able to see the creatures coming now. And the boy would be safe no matter what. "Come on Layne, time to get you home," Allard said. And he led Layne deeper into the tunnel.

As they walked, Allard kept Layne preoccupied by asking him questions about his life, his family, friends. Layne told Allard that his family owned an apple orchard and he had five brothers and sisters. He was the second youngest. His oldest sister, Evaine, was his best friend. She was apparently "old like you", as Layne put it. He liked to play hide and seek in the woods with his sister but he didn't always tell her that he was playing and so it would take her hours to find him.

A few days ago, Layne had been playing in the woods, waiting for his sister to find him, when a dragon landed, knocking over several trees that were very close to his hiding place. Layne wanted to run but he was frozen. Then the dragon drew in a great breath and, in a voice so loud it hurt his ears, said "I smell something delicious." The dragon turned toward him and Layne had run.

The entrance to the Tunnel of Interminable Suffering had been unmanned. Generally, there was a kind old man there, who put up with Layne's thousands of questions, guarding the entrance, warning people away. But the man was gone and so Layne had run straight into the entrance of the tunnel.

The dragon almost got him. As he'd been running to the entrance of the tunnel, the dragon snapped at Layne's feet, but only his snout could fit into the entrance. He unfurled his long forked tongue to try and snatch Layne up. But Layne had been able to escape far enough into the tunnel so even the dragon's tongue couldn't reach him. He'd waited until he heard the dragon leave, before trying to work his way back the way he'd come. But everything was different and Layne had quickly gotten lost.

"Then those things started chasing me and sometimes I'd lose them but they'd always-always find me," the boy said, on the verge of tears again.

"Did I tell you why I'm in this tunnel? Where I'm going?" Allard said.

"No," Layne said.

"I'm going to slay the very dragon who chased you in here."

"Really?" Layne asked, he sounded deeply impressed, and unconsciously huddled closer to the prince.

"Yes. I'm on a quest. Just like Allard of the Green."

"I thought that was your name," Layne said.

"He's who I'm named after. Have you really never heard of Allard of the Green? From the Shining Era?"

Layne responded in the negative. So Allard kept Layne entertained, as well as he could considering his admittedly dry storytelling skills, by telling him tales of Allard of the Green, and how the Green defeated the dragon Enfanalda and her eight headed son Griskelion. He told Layne how the Green became a great general who had the undying loyalty of his men, because the Green offered to fight the opposing commander in single combat before every battle so as to avoid the unnecessary bloodshed of men on both sides. Occasionally the opposing commander would take him up on the offer and be swiftly defeated. But when they refused, their men were so disheartened to learn that their commander wouldn't die for them that the Green and his men defeated them easily. The Green knew every one of his soldier's names and often visited those on night watch. He'd invented the code by which knights were supposed to live, though Allard knew few bothered anymore. But Allard still did his best to live by the Code of the Green. It had served him well thus far.

Their vision began to fade, and they had to pause briefly to drink more of the Water of the Cave-mers.

When Allard could see properly again, a large sickly pale green reptilian creature with a disturbingly human body was coming up the tunnel, heading straight for him and moving alarmingly fast. Allard pushed Layne behind him and cut down the creature with his sword. The creature's momentum carried it crashing into Allard and it collapsed on top of him, dead.

Allard struggled under the creature's great weight but couldn't shift the carcass. Layne tried to help, but he was too small to make any sort of difference.

Allard tried again to roll the creature off of him but it was no use. Then he remembered the ring. He'd already used most of the more common insects. But he knew of some obscure ones as well. If he could become small enough, he could just crawl out from under the creature...

He explained the plan to Layne and the boy took to the plan with great zeal. Allard's knowledge of bugs ran out fairly quickly as all of his were already taken. So it fell to Layne, a big fan of all creatures that creep and crawl, to give him suggestions.

"Try backswimmer."

Allard could feel the fungi on the ground growing and moving underneath him. He tried not to shudder but he couldn't help it. He tried the boy's suggestion. "Looks like it's been taken."

"Oh! Bronze beetle. Try bronze beetle," Layne said.

"Sorry kid. Taken."

"Crane fly."

Allard repeated Layne's suggestion and nothing happened.

Allard gritted his teeth in pain. Mycelium burrowed into his skin as a mushroom grew on his shoulder.

They ran through several more options quickly, but Layne's suggestions began to slow as even his encyclopedic knowledge of bugs ran out. Allard dutifully repeated whatever bug the boy gave him, but he was also using the long pauses to come up with a new strategy.

Layne sat in silence, thinking back to all the insects he'd seen or been told about. All the arachnids and worms as well. He thought back to the man who had come from the far west and told him of creatures with shining shells and patterned wings, creatures with many legs and many eyes and some with neither of those things. Layne knew he could remember more. He just knew it. He just had to think. Allard needed him. The man had already taken on mythic proportions in Layne's eyes. He could sword fight and was on a quest and talked like a proper hero. He was just like a character out of one of the stories Evaine told him when he was little. He could help. He just had to *think*.

Finally, Layne lit up with inspiration. "Paper wasp! Paper wasp. Do paper wasp!"

Allard looked up at Layne, winked, and smiled at him encouragingly. "Paper wasp." As he said the words, his body shrank down. Wings sprouted from his back and he grew another set of legs.

Layne shot his hands in the air. "Yes!"

Allard crawled out from under the creature and then flew at Layne's eye level for a moment. Layne stuck out his finger. Allard landed on it, and Layne brought his finger up to his face, so close to his face he was nearly touching the bridge of his own nose that his eyes crossed as , tried to see if the wasp still looked like Allard.

All Allard could see was a gigantic pair of eyes. After a moment, he took off from Layne's finger. Then he let go of the idea of the paper wasp in his mind and changed back into a human.

9

Chapter 9

They walked on, periodically sipping more of the Water of the Cavemers. Occasionally, Allard would have to kill one of the creatures, but they were stupid and easily dispatched.

Then they came to yet another fork in the tunnel. Allard turned to take the left fork but he smacked into the cave wall as he stepped forward, bloodying his forehead. He stared in front of him in consternation. The tunnel looked completely open, with no visible obstructions, but when he put out his hand to feel in front of him, there was solid rock. He now knew how Layne had injured his face.

Allard looked down at Layne, to poke fun at them both, saying that they matched now, but he saw that Layne's mouth was moving, but no sound was coming out.

"What?" Allard said. Except he made no sound either.

Layne kept talking, but Allard still had no idea what he was saying. Allard realized that the only sound he could hear was the constant grinding as the Morphing Mountain moved overhead. And that noise was growing louder all the time.

"Can you hear me?" he yelled to Layne.

Layne nodded and tried to talk.

"I'm sorry Layne. It's too loud in here. Can you yell?"

Layne yelled. But Allard still couldn't hear him.

Allard knelt down so Layne could speak directly into his ear. Still nothing. Then, he had Layne yell into his ear. Nothing. It had finally happened. Allard was deaf. He could hear nothing. Nothing except that constant maddening grinding of the moving mountain.

Allard took Layne's hand. "You shake my hand like this—" he shook Layne's hand back and forth rapidly "—if you need to tell me something, alright?"

They walked hand in hand down the tunnel. Every once in a while, Allard would begin walking down a dead end, the tunnel tricking him into thinking it was a clear passage, but then Layne would shake his hand and Allard would stop to look at him questioningly. Layne would point at the dead end then pretend to smack himself in the forehead. Allard would nod and they would continue down the correct path.

There was no more talk of Layne's family or tales of Allard the Green. They walked in grim silence.

The grinding of the mountain grew louder and louder. Allard tried to think about something else, trying not to wonder if the deafness was permanent. He tried to focus on the glowing fungi sprouting from the tunnel walls instead. How beautiful the illustrations would be when he mapped the tunnel. Great big pink oyster shell mushrooms. Jolly little red caps. Frilly yellow chanterelles. Little ghostly caps on delicate stems.

Layne was doing his best to be brave but he knew the tunnel had more tricks in store, things he hadn't thought to warn Allard about, and now he couldn't. Soon, Allard would begin to see things the way Layne had when he'd thought he'd seen his dad and sister wandering the tunnel looking for him, though he knew now that it hadn't been real. He should have warned Allard...

The weight of the silence threatened to crush Layne. He sang quiet little songs to himself to banish it.

But soon enough, Layne gave up on the songs. They weren't helping, and he was getting out of breath as Allard moved faster and faster through the tunnel.

Then Layne almost smacked into Allard's back as Allard drew to an abrupt halt.

54

"What?" Allard said.

"I didn't say anything," Layne said.

"Who's there?" Allard asked. He looked all around and pulled out his sword.

"Allard. Who are you talking to?" Cold dread settled in Layne's stomach. It was starting. He should have warned Allard.

Allard ignored him, still acting like he couldn't hear him. Instead, his face melted into relief. He let go of Layne's hand and sheathed his sword.

"Dwennon," Allard said into the air. "You fixed my hearing. But how did you get here?"

Layne grabbed Allard's hand and shook it rapidly but Allard didn't pay him any mind.

"Really? You brought him here? But-he wanted to see me that badly?"

"Allard," Layne said. "There's no one there."

"Something he wants to tell me. Do you think it's—" Allard cut himself off with a disbelieving laugh. "Do you think maybe he—"

Whatever Allard wanted to ask the apparition, he could not quite bring himself to say the words, as if worried the possibility would disappear should he speak it aloud.

"There's no one there! The tunnel is tricking you!" Layne yelled.

"Yes. Please. Take me to him," Allard said. He started to walk down a tunnel that branched off from the main path.

Layne wrapped both hands around Allard's wrist. He dug in his heels, doing his best to slow Allard down, but Allard just kept walking. He didn't seem to notice the weight hanging off his arm. Then Layne tripped and fell, but he kept his grip on Allard. Allard dragged him for a few feet before Layne couldn't hold on any longer. He let go and then sprung to his feet. He couldn't stop Allard, but he could follow him and make sure he didn't get hurt.

Allard had never been so happy to see anyone in his life as he was to see Dwennon, who was standing in the middle of the tunnel. The wiley old wizard had so many tricks up his sleeve. More than even Allard knew. He wondered how exactly the wizard had managed to transport his father into the tunnel as well. But he didn't dwell on it. His father had come all this way just to see him.

Layne followed along behind Allard and Dwennon, smiling. He chattered away with Dwennon as they walked. It pleased Allard to see them getting along so well.

"You're going to meet the king," Allard said.

Layne jumped. This was the first time Allard had spoken in an hour. "What?"

"You're going to meet my father. The king. But you musn't worry. He'll like you."

Layne was worried, but not for the reason Allard thought. "Your father isn't here. Allard. We have to stop. This isn't the way out. We're getting lost," Layne said.

Allard smiled as Layne told him how excited he was to meet Allard's father. Then, Dwennon told him that they were nearly there. His father was in the chamber up ahead.

Allard entered the chamber. It was huge, with a high ceiling. A natural skylight at its highest point allowed a bar of moonlight to shine into the chamber, illuminating it. The entire chamber was encrusted with goldenrod lichen. And in the center, sat his father on a throne of mossy rock.

"Father!" Allard cried.

Layne watched helplessly as Allard rushed forward and knelt in front of a large rock.

Allard looked up at his father. "Dwennon said you had something you wanted to tell me."

"Yes," King Cederic said. "Give up."

"What? No," Allard said. He crept forward on his knees. "Father-"

"How could you be so foolish?" his father said. "How could you possibly think I would make you king?"

"No. You said if I slayed Balsinew that I would be king," Allard said.

"I sent you on a fool's errand and prayed you would be killed in the attempt," his father spat.

"He's going to kill you, and I'll be glad," Braxton said as he emerged from the shadows.

Allard ignored his brother's words. Instead, he pleaded with his father. "But

I thought—I'm your son."

His father threw back his head and laughed. His laughter echoed off the chamber walls and multiplied.

"You are no son of mine," his father said. And even though this statement was quieter, it bounced around the room even longer.

The king settled a hand on Braxton's shoulder. "Your brother is my heir. It was never going to be you."

"Never ever ever ever," Braxton said in a sickening singsong voice.

"You said—" Allard began.

"Hey everybody! The freak that would be king!" Braxton yelled.

A crowd of people emerged from the shadows, all the sneering faces of court. They clapped and cheered and pointed and laughed.

"You're too stupid to be king," his brother said.

"You're too weak to be king," his father said.

"Face it, you would have been terrible," Braxton said.

Allard swiped under his eyes with the back of his hand. He kept his head ducked down. He was crumbling under the weight of their words.

"Tears?" the king smirked.

"I want to make an alliance with the barbarians to the west. I shall marry you off to their prince," Braxton said. "Or perhaps that swamp king to the south. You'd like that, wouldn't you?"

"King's don't cry," Cederic said.

His brother placed a hand on Allard's shoulder, a mockery of a comforting gesture. Allard viciously threw his hand off.

Layne rubbed his hand, he'd tried to reach out to comfort Allard, but the prince had slapped it away. So Layne pressed his back to the chamber wall and watched on.

Braxton and his father loomed over him, spitting their venom down at him.

"You're not man enough to be king," his father said.

"You'll never be my brother."

"You'll never be my *son.*"

These final words hit Allard like a physical blow. He curled over on himself, trying to keep his heart from breaking apart.

"Why don't I just finish him off, father?" Braxton asked. He drew a dagger from his pocket; it glinted in the moonlight.

Allard staggered to his feet and drew his sword. "Stay back!"

But Braxton was quick, and he ducked behind Allard. Allard whirled around and struck out at him.

Layne screamed and ducked out of the way as Allard wildly swung his sword at him. Layne tried to find a way to get past the blindly rampaging prince, but his every route was either blocked or fraught with danger. Even if he did get away from Allard, he was still trapped in the tunnel.

Braxton easily dodged Allard's attack. He stabbed at Allard with the dagger. Allard knocked it out of the way.

"I don't want to hurt you," Allard said. He circled Braxton warily. "Put down the dagger."

"I don't have a dagger. Allard. Please!" Layne cried, though of course Allard could not hear him. He was too scared to move, and so he stood, trembling, and waiting for what the prince would do next.

"Braxton. Please," Allard said, his face contorted into a mask of grief. "You don't have to do this. The throne is yours. I'll go. I'll just go."

Layne watched as Allard cringed and blocked an invisible attacker. The blade of his sword passed so close to Layne's face that Layne could feel the air sliced in front of him.

Braxton capered about the chamber, singing a little tune. "I'm going to kill you and he'll be glad." He danced and twirled. "I'm going to kill you and he'll be glad."

Allard's face darkened with anger and Layne cringed away. Allard sheathed his sword. He lunged forward and grabbed Layne by the front of his shirt. He lifted Layne off the ground and shook him.

"Let me go!" Layne screamed. He kicked at Allard.

"Let me go!" Braxton screamed. He kicked at Allard.

Allard slammed Layne into the wall of the chamber. He wrapped his hand around Layne's throat.

"I don't want to hurt you!" Allard screamed in Layne's face. "I'll let you go and you leave me be!"

Layne scratched at Allard's hand, trying to get free. He couldn't breathe.

Braxton glared at Allard with his glittering black eyes, there was nothing in them but pure hatred. Even if he left, his brother wouldn't be content until he was dead.

Layne's vision darkened around the edges. His kicks grew feeble. Going against his instincts to keep prying Allard's fingers from his throat, Layne reached down and ripped the flower from where it was pinned over his heart. He nearly dropped it, but managed to hold on. He pressed the flower to Allard's chest, right over his heart.

Allard looked around the chamber in confusion. Just moments ago, the chamber had been filled with crowds of jeering people, now it was silent except for his own breathing. The walls had been the most vibrant gold and were now just cruel grey rock. His father had been sitting on a beautiful mossy throne, but his father was gone, and the throne simply a pale stone. His brother had been—

Allard turned and saw who exactly he had pinned to the chamber wall—not his brother, but Layne. With a horrified gasp, he let go of Layne's throat.

Layne collapsed to the ground, coughing and gagging.

He could have killed him. He could have *killed* him. Allard dropped to his knees.

The flower fell between them, leaving them both vulnerable.

"I'm so—Layne, I'm so sorry," Allard said.

Layne reached down and picked up the flower. He held it out to Allard.

Allard shook his head. "No. You have it back."

The boy didn't look at Allard, just shook the flower, meaning "take it", meaning Layne was safer with the monsters.

10

Chapter 10

Allard felt a deep shame as he took his flower from Layne's hand and pinned it back over his heart. He picked the boy up and carried him out of the chamber. He carried Layne with his legs wrapped around Allard's waist and his arms around Allard's neck. Allard hoped that if they were close enough together, the flower's protection might extend to them both.

Every once in a while, the boy, in a raspy and broken voice, would tell Allard when a creature was coming, and he would cut it down with his sword, but besides that there was very little talk. Allard carried Layne for a couple hours, not wanting to stop. But eventually, Allard had to take a break. His legs were trembling from the weight of carrying both the boy and his pack.

Allard sat the boy down and knelt in front of him and again pinned the flower to Layne's chest.

The boy tried to refuse it, but Allard insisted. He was already ashamed he'd kept it as long as he had.

With that task complete, Allard sank down and sat with his back braced against the tunnel wall. They had nearly run out of the water of the Cavemers. They only had enough for a few more hours of walking. He dreaded to think what would happen if they ran out before they made it to the end of the tunnel.

And then there was the question of what he would do once he did make it through the tunnel and returned Layne to his family. His father and brother may have only been apparitions, but they told the truth: his father was never going to make him king. They expected him to fail, and even if he succeeded he still wouldn't be king.

His father was not a great king. Allard had known this even before Dwennon pointed it out to him. Cedric was stubborn, more interested in slaying monsters than running a kingdom. He chose only advisors who agreed with him. He was old fashioned. He would not be the one to buck tradition, to take a risk on something new. Allard had known all this. He had accepted it. But then Dwennon had said his father could be persuaded, so Allard had been blinded to these truths. And he'd set off on this ridiculous journey. But even if by some miracle Allard did slay the dragon, his father would never acknowledge him. Fate wasn't on his side. He had no destiny. He was foolish to ever believe he had.

Well, he didn't believe it anymore. It was time to abandon such childish things. Allard would take Layne back to his family, give the flower to Wendla's husband with his apologies for not returning it to her himself, and head east, to work as a hired sword. He knew Dwennon would be disappointed and angry, and would probably never forgive him. But Allard had to be free to live as himself. If he went back, Braxton would punish him. For having the audacity to challenge the king's true heir for the throne. He couldn't do it. He wouldn't.

They kept walking. Allard never let go of Layne's hand. There were whispers in the darkness, but no other blatant attacks.

Then slowly, so slowly Allard could scarcely believe it, the darkness of the tunnel began to fade. The bright orange of sunrise shot into the tunnel. They'd walked all day and all night, but they'd made it.

Layne broke into a wide smile. He dropped Allard's hand and ran toward the exit.

"Layne careful!" Allard yelled, but even in his foul mood he couldn't help the smile of relief that spread across his face.

Layne launched himself out of the tunnel. Allard mustered the last of his energy and broke into a trot to follow him.

When Allard exited the tunnel, he saw Layne wrapped in the arms of an old but hale man with a large colorful knitted cap.

"Ohhh Layne, you know better than to go in the tunnel. I was so worried when that dragon came," the old man said.

"He almost got me!" Layne said. "I had to go in there to get away from him."

The old man squeezed him again, then turned to Allard. "Thank you for bringing him back. I'm afraid I've done a rather poor job guarding the entrance."

The old man shook Allard's hand.

"I believe I met your wife. On the other side," Allard said.

"Wendla!" the old man said. "How is my love?"

"Still doing her best to save fools like me," Allard said. "She asked me to tell you 'the crows are about.'"

The old man leaned forward. "How did she seem? When she said it. Wistful? Or more… mischievous?"

Allard considered for a moment. "Mischievous."

A smile curled across the old man's face as he stared into the distance. "Excellent." Then he turned his attention back to Allard. "I'm Maurice."

"Allard."

"Pleasure," Maurice said.

Allard leaned down and took the flower from Layne's shirt. He handed it to Maurice. "Your wife's."

Maurice gaped. The flower was a family heirloom, hundreds of years old. Wendla would never lend it to a stranger. If she gave it to this man, it was with good reason.

Maurice curled Allard's fingers back around the flower. "You hold onto it. For the return journey."

Allard agreed and put it in his bag for safe keeping. He would explain to Maurice that he wasn't going back later. He would make sure Maurice took the flower back, but he had no desire to discuss that in front of Layne.

"I had better get Layne here back to his family, I think they've worried rather long enough," Allard said.

Maurice had a funny look on his face after Allard mentioned Layne's family, and looked like he wanted to call after them. But he didn't, and Layne and Allard continued on through the woods.

Eventually the pine trees gave way to apple trees as they reached the border of Layne's family's orchard. But instead of the neat little rows of trees Layne had seen all his life, devastation greeted them. Trees were torn down and uprooted. The barn was a blackened husk, the ground rended open into great messy furrows.

Layne ran toward the house. "Mama! Papa!"

There was no answer. Allard chased after him.

"Mama! Papa! Evaine!"

Then a woman with dark hair in a long thick braid came out of the house. She saw the boy and screamed "Layne!"

She ran down the stairs and scooped Layne up in her arms. She covered him in kisses.

"Mama!" Layne wailed.

"Oh Layne. My baby." She squeezed him hard. "Anders! Layne's back!"

"Mila?" Layne's father, Anders, a large, blond, bearded man, ran around from the front of the house, calling his wife's name. He nearly bowled his wife and Layne clean over. He hugged Layne. His hand rested on the back of Layne's head as Layne sobbed into his neck.

"Oh, my boy, oh, my boy," Anders said. It seemed to be all he could say.

Now that Layne was reunited with his family, Allard could quietly slip away and start his new life. But before he could, Layne gestured back toward him.

Allard waved at Layne's parents but made no move to come closer.

Layne wiggled around until his father set him down. Then he marched over and grabbed Allard's hand. "This is the man who saved me," Layne said, as he dragged Allard back toward his parents.

The man who had barely saved him. The man who, in fact, had almost killed him. Allard could see the bruises already forming on Layne's neck. He was no savior.

"He fought this monster that was trying to get me. And then he fought this other monster that was really big and heavy but was invisible. And then he used magic to turn into a wasp. And—"

63

Layne was interrupted by his siblings, who were running out of the house. But there was no sign of Evaine, only his little sister and three older brothers.

Layne paused in his story. He wanted to make sure Evaine heard it. Maybe she'd be impressed and fall in love with Allard. That Allard would fall in love with Evaine was already a foregone conclusion in Layne's mind. Layne hugged his other siblings but kept his eyes glued on the door, waiting for Evaine.

But Evaine didn't follow the others. She didn't come out.

"Where's Evaine?" Layne asked.

His parents exchanged a glance.

"Where is she?"

"Layne. She—" Mila broke off. Couldn't answer him.

"Where is she?!"

Allard watched the scene unfold with a pit in his stomach. He knew what Maurice had been unable to say. "Where is she?!" Layne yelled.

"Taken," Anders said. "Taken by the dragon."

Layne's face crumpled as he dissolved into tears. "What?"

"When you didn't come home, and the dragon attacked, she got worried. She went to go look for you and one of the men, one of the men from town saw the dragon flying away. And he had Evaine." The last syllable of Evaine's name was very high coming out of Ander's mouth. He was doing his best not to cry. "He took our girl. And I thought he ate you."

Layne hugged his father. "It's going to be okay. Allard will get her back. He's going to slay the dragon." Layne turned back toward Allard. "Aren't you?"

Layne looked so hopeful, so sure that Allard would be able to defeat the dragon. Allard didn't have the heart to tell Layne that his plans had changed. Allard was running. It was shameful enough that he was doing it without adding to the pain by explaining his moral failings to a seven year old.

Then he looked to Layne's parents. They wore the same hopeful expressions. Allard couldn't even look Layne's mother in the eye. She had dark eyes like his own mother. It was shocking how similar hope and terror looked as both played across Mila's face.

"Could you really get her back?" Mila asked.

Allard couldn't extinguish that hope.

There was a small chance that the girl might still be alive. Dragons didn't always eat their captives right away. They liked to toy with them first, use them for entertainment, and then, once they were bored, they had a meal. Allard had spent many nights wondering how long Balsinew had kept his mother as entertainment, or whether she angered him enough that he had eaten her quickly. Allard didn't know which was worse.

There was little to be accomplished by Allard attempting to slay the dragon. He would most likely be killed in the attempt and even if he did succeed, he wouldn't be king. But perhaps he could sneak into Balsinew's lair, rescue Evaine, if she was still alive, and sneak back out.

Then, *then*, he could begin his new life in the east.

A voice in the back of Allard's head that, annoyingly, sounded a lot like Dwennon, pointed out that even if he didn't become king, the world would still be a better place with Balsinew dead. He ignored this voice.

"Yes. I will do all I can to bring her home."

Mila grabbed her husband's hand and brought it to her chest.

"Thank you," Anders said.

11

Chapter 11

Mila put out a veritable feast for breakfast: bacon and eggs and hotcakes and apple cider. It was the best apple cider Allard had ever tasted and he had four cups. Layne wolfed down everything within reach. Though as the meal progressed, he slowed down considerably, until he wasn't engaging in conversation at all, just blinking slowly while methodically shoving hotcakes with apple jam into his mouth, not bothering to chew.

Mila noted this with a fond smile. She hadn't thought she'd see her baby boy ever again. She didn't think she'd ever get to laugh as he "helped" her with the laundry by keeping her entertained with odd stories he made up about worms. She had thought she'd never again scold him for talking with his mouth full, or getting grass stains on his church trousers, or forgetting to water the horse, that she'd never again run her fingers through his sunny-straw hair. But her baby boy was back. And he was exhausted.

"I think it's time for Layne to get some rest," Mila said. "And Allard as well."

"Mmnot even tired," Layne said.

"I might have believed you if you'd opened your eyes," Mila said. "To bed with you."

Layne lifted up his arms expectantly. Anders stood and picked up his boy and carried him back toward his room.

Allard stood. "I should be off."

Mila put her hand on his shoulder. "Rest. For a while."

"The sooner I get there, the sooner—"

"You're dead on your feet. It'll do no good if you fall asleep on the dragon's doorstep, yes?"

Until this moment, Allard had not allowed himself to feel just how tired he really was, walking all day and night, carrying Layne for great stretches, the stress and fear. He was worn to the bone. "Thank you. Ma'am."

Mila surprised him by throwing her arms around his neck. Allard froze, unsure what to do with his hands for a moment, but eventually returned the hug.

"Thank you. Thank you thank you thank you," Mila murmured. Then she led him to her eldest son's room.

"Just a few hours," Allard said. Then, he fell into a deep dreamless sleep.

He was awakened by Layne diving onto the bed and bouncing up and down. Allard sat up and wiped the sleep out of his eyes.

"Are you going to rescue my sister now?"

Layne casually climbed all over Allard, the same way Allard had seen him do with his brothers at breakfast. So, Allard copied them and grabbed Layne by the ankle. He stood up and held Layne upside down by his foot. Layne giggled. Allard pulled Layne up as close to his face as he could, still holding him up by his foot.

"Yes. I'm going to rescue your sister now."

Allard flung Layne onto the bed. He walked out the door but paused in the doorway. "Want to help me with my armor? Squire?"

Layne launched himself out of the bed and followed Allard out of the room.

Allard retrieved his bag from outside and sat under an apple tree to prepare. First, he sharpened his sword. Then he pulled out a mail shirt and pulled it on over his head. Next, he had Layne help him with the buckles on his chestplate. He removed the spool of unicorn thread from his pack and stuck it in his pocket. He didn't know what state he would find Evaine in, but there was nothing better than unicorn hair if she was hurt.

Soon, he was ready to go. Layne's parents gave him their horse to use. She was an old nag but they told him that she could still move pretty quickly if the need arose.

Layne ran up and wrapped his arms around Allard's waist. "I know you'll get her back."

Allard knelt down so he could hug Layne properly. "I will."

Then Allard climbed onto the old mare's back, clicked at her with his mouth and was off to face the dragon.

As Allard rode, he passed by a village that had been devastated by Balsinew. Buildings were still smoldering. People wandered the streets, not even sure where to begin rebuilding. Feeling like a coward, Allard kept his eyes to the road.

Balsinew made no secret of where his lair was. It was a deep cave set into a large hillside in the forest. He invited any who would challenge him to come in the front door. He had nothing to fear.

After riding about an hour through the forest, Allard came upon the entrance to Balsinew's lair. He had no idea if Balsinew was inside or not. He decided to wait and see if there was any movement at the mouth of the cave.

He did not have to wait long. He heard the rumble of Balsinew's voice and saw the way it startled all of the birds in the forest into flight.

The rumble grew louder as Balsinew made his way toward the exit of the cave.

Allard thought that his childhood memories had enlarged Balsinew, but the size of the dragon was still awesome in the most literal sense of the term. The ground shook when he walked. His head peeked through some of the lower hanging clouds. How had the Allard of the Green ever slain something like that?

With a few beats of his powerful wings, the dragon took flight. He flew toward the mountains to the south.

Allard wasted no time. He tied up his horse and then quickly climbed the hillside to the entrance of the cave.

There was a huge tunnel that led into the main cavern. For Allard it was quite a long passage, but for the dragon it was mere steps away.

The tunnel opened up into the main cavern. The ceiling was very high, as if it nearly reached the peak of the hilltop. Large rock structures studded the cavern, which was lit with torches. There were piles of jewels and gold and furniture and books and food and art. Ropes, festooned with hanging bird cages, dropped from the ceiling. Canopies and tapestries hung from the walls of the cavern. Everything was precariously stacked but meticulously organized.

Allard carefully picked his way through the treasure, wondering where he should start looking for Evaine.

"Careful. He sets traps," a voice called down.

12

Chapter 12

Allard looked up and saw a tall, skinny rock pedestal. On top of the pedestal sat a woman encased in glass, with only her head and neck free; Balsinew must have used his fire to fashion a blown glass prison. The woman was forced to remain frozen as if in the midst of a graceful dance move. One foot stretched in the air behind her, and her arms were held out in an elegant sweep in front of her. The glass twirled and swirled around her in thick tendrils that ended in sharp points to dissuade anyone from getting too close.

"Are you a treasure hunter?" the woman asked.

She'd seen three treasure hunters meet their doom already and she'd only been the dragon's prisoner for 4 days. The dragon purposefully left his lair and his incredible hoard unguarded to entice bandits to come try their hand while they thought he was out hunting. In actuality, he had magical little bells rigged up amongst his piles of antique furniture and chests of gold and jewels and fine fabrics. The bells seemed quiet but their sound could actually be heard for miles. A man with gold pieces in his eyes would accidentally ring the bell and think nothing of it, not knowing the dragon hid nearby, waiting for someone to spring his trap. Whenever someone rang the bell, Balsinew would hurry back in for a bit of midday sport.

Not one of the treasure hunters she'd watched the dragon eat had even attempted to rescue her. It had put quite a damper on her formerly-optimistic outlook on humanity. After the first two had roundly ignored her pleas for help, she hadn't even bothered calling out to the third. She just listlessly tried to help him navigate as many of the traps as she could remember. She just wanted *someone* to escape. But eventually, he had set off one of those little bells and the dragon was on him in an instant. And now, this new man had arrived.

"No. Not a treasure hunter," Allard said. "I'm here to rescue you."

"Oh my days, that sounded very good," the woman said. Except that the man didn't seem like he was just trying to *sound* good, not in the way she'd seen in many a too handsome for his own good boy in the village. He seemed very serious, a bit stiff. And he spoke slowly, very carefully considering each word.

"Evaine, right?" Allard said.

"How do you know my name?" Evaine asked.

"Layne sent me."

All of Evaine's wry detachment disappeared in an instant. "Layne? Layne's alive?"

Allard nodded. "Yes. He got chased into the Tunnel of Interminable Suffering and got lost."

"And you brought him home."

"Yes," Allard said.

Evaine smiled widely and burst into tears at the same time. "Well then, you better get to rescuing me then," she said, attempting a normal sounding voice.

She could see his blush even from her high perch.

Allard ran through a list of flying insects Layne had given him, "just in case." Finally, he he uttered the words "blackberry looper"and transformed into a moth.

He fluttered up until he reached Evaine's pedestal. When he changed back into a human, there was barely enough room for him to stand without either falling off the edge or getting impaled by one of the glass tendrils that surrounded her.

"Well, that is quite a trick," Evaine said. In the time it had taken Allard to fly up to her, she had already gotten her emotions back under control.

Allard was finally close enough to get a proper look at Evaine. She had long, thick black hair and dark, soulful eyes. He could see her resemblance to Layne—they both had the same nose, a nose that looked a bit like it had been broken. She looked strong from a lifetime working her family's orchard. She was the most beautiful woman Allard had ever seen.

Evaine caught him staring and smirked at him. "I believe we were in the midst of a rescue attempt?"

Allard nodded. "Of course. Terribly sorry. I'll get you out of here."

"Well. As long as you are *terribly* sorry…" Evaine said. She had not had much occasion to smile in the last days, not much occasion to feel hopeful, but she did feel hopeful now. She was almost giddy with it. There was something about this man that made her believe him when he spoke.

Allard could only look at her smile for a moment, otherwise he'd never be able to concentrate. He circled Evaine's glass prison, trying to find the best way to free her from it. He didn't speak, just considered all the options.

"What's your name?" Evaine asked.

"Allard," he answered.

"New to speaking? Allard?"

Allard glanced up at her from where he had kneeled down to examine the glass around her feet. She was smiling again.

"Hm? Oh. No," he said.

"You're being awfully quiet. Care to share your findings?" She was, once again frustrated by her severely limited movement, if she'd been free she would have reached out to brush his arm and get his attention.

Allard removed the menagerie ring from his finger and held it up for her before slipping it back on. "If I can get your hand free, I thought we might use this," he said. "You can turn into an animal small enough to get free." It had worked well enough last time. It could work again, so long as they were able to come up with another tiny creature. The list was already getting quite short.

"And how do you plan on getting my hand free?" Evaine asked.

"Unfortunately, you are all caught up," Allard said. "I haven't yet found a solution. Any ideas?"

Evaine tilted her head this way and that, as much as she was able, looking for anything that might help. Then she spotted a hammer amongst the dragon's pile of weaponry.

"There's a hammer down there," Evain said. She, of course, could not point to it but after several minutes of saying "a little to the right, no, too far," she did manage to help him spot it.

The hammer would certainly be more effective than having Allard chop away at the glass with his sword. "And get one of those rugs as well," Evaine said. "Keep the glass from cutting us both to ribbons."

After several attempts, Allard turned into the largest bird he could think of, a type of stork called a Great Adjutant, and flew down to gather the hammer and a rug. All of the rugs were too heavy, even for a bird so large, and so he had to settle for some thick but pliable fabric, which took him several minutes to find. It was the longest he'd been able to retain animal form, and he feared turning back into a human midair. But he managed to make it back to the pedestal with the necessary supplies.

He laid the fabric over the first of the large tendrils of glass, then gently tapped the hammer against it. The sharp point snapped off, dropping at his feet. Slowly and carefully, he continued to break the glass. Every once in a while, Allard would check on Evaine, but besides that he said very little. And so Evaine was left to carry on the conversation.

It suited her. Evaine tended to talk when she was nervous, a quality the dragon apparently found entertaining. She was certain the dragon only kept her around to hear her ramble on any number of subjects so as to avoid thought of her predicament.

So Evaine told Allard stories about Layne and her other siblings. She told him the story of how her parents met, a quietly sweet tale in which their eyes met at a baking contest at the local fair in which they were considered the favorites.

She told him of her time with the dragon, how he had given her food, and jewels to wear, but when she tried to escape, he placed her in the glass prison as a punishment. He thought it was funny to make "such a sturdy young lass" pose like a ballerina. The dragon would disappear for hours and return with the strangest things: bright, colorful paintings, elaborate tapestries snatched from palace walls, clothes he couldn't wear, furniture he couldn't use, musical instruments he couldn't play, all of them stunningly beautiful.

The dragon would also occasionally take her out to "play." He would have her dig through trunks upon trunks of the finest clothes, to build outfits, which he would then have her try on. When she came out from behind the changing screen wearing a long purple ball gown, the dragon would ask her to spin. Then he would command Evaine to try on the yellow opera singer's costume or the ermine cloak or the dress festooned with feathers.

Evaine stopped speaking when she noticed Allard's harsh breathing. He gripped the hammer so tightly his knuckles had gone white and his hand was trembling.

"Allard? What is it? What's the matter?"

Allard shook his head and continued working. "It doesn't matter. We're getting close. I have to focus."

"Please tell me," she said.

Her voice was so soft Allard had no choice but to look up at her. And he saw nothing but kindness in her eyes. "My mother was taken. By Balsinew. Many years ago."

Allard tapped at the glass with the hammer. He'd nearly reached her finger tips. Then he would have to be careful not to crack the glass too hard lest he cut her hand.

"I'm so sorry, Allard," Evaine said.

"I just wonder… if that's what he made her do. Dress up like a little dolly." For the first time, Allard considered that if he failed to free Evaine and was caught, the dragon might not kill him, might instead want to keep him.

Evaine asked Allard more questions. Eventually, she drew the whole story from him, his father and brother and the dragon, about how he was a prince and hoped one day to be king, Dwennon's gifts, the ring, the spool of unicorn hair thread in his pocket, Prism Valley and the tunnel. He apologized to her for failing to protect her brother properly. She pointed out that her brother surely would have been dead without him.

And as Allard spoke, Evaine began to fall in love with him, as preposterous as that was, for a farmer's daughter to fall in love with a prince. But she could hold this idea in her heart. No one else need know about it.

Finally, Allard freed Evaine's hand enough that he could slip the ring over her finger. They read off the rest of the list of crawlers Layne had given Allard, but all had been taken.

Allard sat on the edge of the pedestal, his feet dangling. He tried to remember every strange and exotic creature Dwennon had ever told him about. Evaine dredged up every single conversation she'd ever had with her little brother about the slimy creepy crawlies he loved so much.

Their guesses, which had not come quickly to begin with, dwindled down to nothing.

Allard ran his fingers through his hair until it stood up in lunatic peaks as he thought. Then he climbed onto his knees and set to work breaking Evaine free with the hammer. It was slow work but at least he could get her out that way.

"Stop," Evaine said.

"I can get you free," Allard said.

"Not before he comes back. We've been too long already. If you keep at that, he'll see. He'll know you're here."

"He'll know I am here anyway because I will be standing here," Allard said.

"So he can kill you instantly and take the ring?" Evaine asked.

The walls of the cavern shuddered. The ground shook and Allard was nearly thrown from the pedestal.

"He's coming back. You have to hide," Evaine said.

"No. I can protect you." He stubbornly set his jaw.

"You have to go now. You have to start climbing. If he finds you then we are both dead."

Allard hesitated.

"Go! Now!" Evaine commanded.

Allard reached out and gently touched her free hand, then began the long climb down from the tall stone pedestal. The ground shook harder, knocking rocks free from the ceiling and walls. Allard clung tightly to the spire to avoid falling and crashing into a garden of marble statues below.

13

Chapter 13

The dragon entered the cavern, with Allard still fifteen feet off the ground, clinging to the spire. He dropped the last little distance and had to land on his feet, rather than tucking and rolling. He couldn't risk knocking over any of the statues.

"Ah, the mighty hunter has returned," Evaine called out, to divert the dragon's attention from the floor of the cavern.

"Nooooo longer giving me the silent treatment hmmmm?" the dragon said. His voice was so deep and loud it made Evaine's glass prison rattle. Balsinew slinked toward her, delicately stepping over and around his piles of treasure. Despite his size, he never knocked anything over, too in love with his beautiful belongings. And Evaine was his prize item of the moment, so long as she kept proving...*interesting.*

"Guess I missed you," Evaine said. It took all of her concentration not to glance downward to check on Allard's progress.

Allard quickly and quietly weaved his way out of the statue garden. He carefully picked his way over a mountain of fine shoes, which was all that stood behind him and a small natural tunnel that burrowed into the cave wall. From there, he would be hidden but still have a good view of Evaine and the dragon.

Evaine made sure to keep her fingers stiff and outstretched, trying to not draw attention to the chipped-away glass and the ring. If she could avoid detection until the dragon flopped down on his bed made of a thousand feather mattresses, then she would have the night to find one creature that hadn't been used by the blasted ring before. She had to wonder exactly what was the point of a ring where you could only become a creature once; it seemed unnecessarily inconvenient.

"So what have you brought back today?" Evaine asked.

"Why allllll the sudden innnterest?" Balsinew asked.

"Like I said. Bored. Staring at a cave wall for hours is not as exciting as one might think," Evaine said.

The dragon's glittering eyes pored over her face suspiciously, but Evaine maintained her bored look.

Then the dragon broke into a slow curling smile and held up a taxidermied wolf. "Is this not the most lovely thing you've ever seen?"

She was forced to agree that it was indeed stunning, as she had every trinket he had brought back to the cave during her imprisonment.

"And what do you like best about it?" the dragon asked.

Evaine was caught off guard. He'd never asked that before. "What?"

"Your admiration rings false. Soooo what do you like best about it?" Balsinew's tail flicked back and forth.

"His… expression," Evaine said.

The wolf's face was pulled into a snarl, its eyes narrowed in cruel slits.

"His expression," the dragon said. He set aside the wolf, something more interesting had come up.

"Yes," Evaine said.

"Yoooou are acting quite strange today, there is something you're not telling me."

In the little tunnel, Allard slowly pulled his sword from the scabbard, careful not to make a sound.

Evaine struggled to keep her voice neutral. "What could that possibly be? I can't do anything. I'm trapped."

"But there could be someone else here. Is there?" the dragon asked.

"Did you hear one of your little bells ring?" Evaine asked.

"Maybe he's a bit more clever. Maybe he's still herrrrrre." Balsinew took a deep breath, scenting the air. "Where is he?"

"I can't magic someone out of thin air," Evaine said, her voice disappearing into a squeak.

"You'll tell me." Balsinew reached out one of his massive claws. He nudged Evaine and her glass prison toward the edge of the pedestal, like a bored housecat knocking a cup off a countertop.

Allard couldn't stand and watch anymore. He climbed out from his hiding place. He would fight the dragon and give Evaine time to escape. It was all he could do.

Evaine squeezed her eyes shut. But the dragon kept pushing her closer and closer to the edge, so she opened them again—she had to know how long she had until she toppled over into the statues below. Soon she was perfectly balanced, a glass figurine hanging out over thin air. Any movement would tip her and her prison over the edge and send her plummeting to her death. The dragon tapped her gently. She screamed. The whole structure lurched sickeningly.

Then the dragon pushed her back toward the center of the pedestal. "Where is he?"

"I am here!" Allard yelled. His voice echoed throughout the cavern, sounding almost as loud as the dragon's, if only for a moment. He stood atop a mountain of golden pieces with his sword pointed at the dragon.

The dragon spun around, even in his haste, he still managed to avoid knocking over a single one of his belongings. He looked pleased. "The little prince. After alllll this time." Of course he remembered the princeling. Balsinew never forgot anything. There were times he still thought about his stolen queen. He'd not gotten to play with her as long as he would have liked. She wouldn't allow it.

"Release her, Balsinew," Allard said. He held his ground even as the dragon slithered toward him with that disturbing grace and quickness. He did not stumble back a single inch.

"Mmmmmm, I'm afraid not," the dragon said.

"This is your last chance," the prince said. "Release her and we will leave you in peace. If you do not, then I shall have no choice but to kill you."

The dragon's laughter nearly drove Allard to his knees, just with the sheer force of the sound pressing down on him. But he remained standing.

"Then I suppose you have no choice," the dragon said.

Allard launched himself off the mountain of gold and ran full tilt toward Balsinew, intending to stab him in his withered heart.

Balsinew clawed at him. Without breaking stride, Allard dropped into a shoulder roll and then snapped back to his feet and continued running, adjusting his grip on the hilt of the sword as he moved. His father's sword was heavier than his own, but perfectly balanced. In the short time he'd wielded it, it already felt like an extension of his arm.

Allard took a flying leap and would have connected with the dragon's chest except that Balsinew chose that moment to rear up, protecting his heart, but leaving his pale belly exposed.

Allard cut through Balsinew's leathery skin, drawing brackish green blood. He drove the sword as deeply as he could. Rivulets of blood dripped down the sword, leaving the hilt slick and, as the dragon moved, the blade turned in Allard's hand.

Balsinew shrieked and grabbed at him. The dragon picked Allard up and threw him against the cave wall, careful to avoid hitting any of his towering piles of treasure.

Allard slammed into the wall. His breastplate struck the wall first and absorbed the brunt of the impact. So he was able to quickly scramble to his feet and prepare his next attack. The slit in Balsinew's belly was already beginning to knit back together.

Dragons healed quickly. This was one of the very first things Dwennon ever taught Allard, once he realized how much the subject interested the young prince. It was their greatest advantage, and it made them extremely difficult to kill. But their hide was not difficult to pierce and they could be killed if you overwhelmed them with injuries, effectively overwhelming their ability to heal. This meant that dragons often withdrew from battle if they sensed the tide turning against them. They would leave and regroup, heal, and attack again.

When Allard had first learned this, he'd felt a pang of despair. He had asked Dwennon, "How does anyone kill a dragon?" It seemed impossible, but Dwennon told him if an attacker had the ability to pursue the dragon and continue attacking, they could wear the dragon down and deliver a fatal blow to the heart. The key was to keep driving.

Allard had spent a lot of time training and learning how to use large creatures' size against them, so he was able to dodge Balsinew's attacks and get under the dragon by repeatedly stabbing upward at the dragon's belly. But the dragon took flight, blowing over piles of treasure with the force of the air moving under his beating wings.

Allard watched as all of the dragon's injuries began to heal. The dragon took a great breath. Little licks of flame escaped from between his teeth. Allard ducked down behind a mountain of sapphires, some small polished jewels, others still large and raw as if freshly ripped from the mines. He expected a jet of fire to blast over his head, possibly even through the sapphires. But the dragon let the flame die in his throat.

Evaine watched Allard circle and attack. He weaved between the dragon's legs, slashing and stabbing. All the while, she murmured the names of animals. She'd given up on insects and had moved onto small birds and rodents but still hadn't found one that hadn't been used. The dragon took wing again and erased all of Allard's good work. He was back to where he started. And Evaine could tell Allard was getting tired.

Allard needed to find a way to keep the dragon earthbound. At the far end of the cavern was a curtain of ropes that dropped from the ceiling all the way to the floor. Hundreds of empty gilded birdcages hung from the ropes. If he could drive Balsinew into those ropes, the dragon's wings would be hopelessly tangled and Allard would have him trapped.

Allard delivered a blow to a particularly painful spot under the dragon's arm. Balsinew roared and dropped down, trying to crush Allard underneath him. Allard managed to get out from under the dragon in time, but only just barely. The only route of escape was to run toward the dragon's front, which put him closer to the dragon's mouth than he would have liked.

The dragon flicked out his tongue and wrapped it around Allard's ankle. One of the tines of his forked tongue dragged dead and useless through the dirt. It had died when Queen Belinda had stabbed it—Balsinew had ripped his own tongue in two to free himself. He jerked Allard's feet out from under him before Allard could do anything.

Balsinew started to drag Allard toward his mouth. His tongue was iron hot against Allard's skin, laying fresh burns over old scars. Allard slashed at the dragon's tongue with his sword, but Balsinew kept whipping him around and making it impossible for him to get a clear angle of attack.

Evaine kept saying the names of animals to herself. "White-throated needletail. Alpine swift. Um. Great spotted cuckoo! Ermine! Come on. Barnswallow. Black bellied sandgrouse. Please! Woodmouse. Vole." Something had to work. *Something had to work.*

Allard screamed in pain as Balsinew dragged him toward his great gaping maw.

The fireball in the dragon's throat grew larger as he pulled Allard toward his great furnace of a mouth. Allard grabbed at rocks and treasures. Anything to slow down the inexorable drag toward the dragon's mouth.

"Marmot. Lemming. *Flying squirrel!*" Evaine said, teary desperation working its way into her voice. Allard was going to be killed. She had to do something. Finally, she said, "Sod it. Griffin!"

The glass around Evaine shattered into a great cloud of shimmering dust. She launched herself off the pedestal and fell into a deep dive. Right before she hit the ground, she flapped her wings and pulled out of the dive.

Evaine kept flapping her wings, assuming it would take an enormous amount of power to keep herself aloft because her lioness body was so heavy, but then she looked up and saw the ceiling rushing straight for her.

Evaine tilted her wings, just barely managing to avoid a collision with the stalactite-encrusted ceiling. She could feel how the air traveled under her feathers and she adjusted them minutely to bring herself back around to where the dragon had trapped Allard. With the griffin's powerful eagle eye, she could see the pain twisting Allard's face as he tried and failed to keep himself from being pulled toward the dragon's mouth.

Evaine extended her wings out fully, dragging the air like a hawk swooping down for an attack. She let out a long brutal shriek as she tore at the dragon's snout.

The dragon roared loud enough to rattle her teeth and he released Allard. Evaine looped over and launched herself at the dragon again. She tore at Balsinew's neck with her talons. The dragon wildly shook his head to dislodge her. Balsinew staggered backward.

Evaine flew down low and wrapped her talons around Allard's arms, hauling him aloft. It was a struggle for her to stay airborne, but she beat her wings furiously toward the exit to the cave.

14

Chapter 14

The dragon didn't follow. Allard cast back a few glances over his shoulder. His ribs twinged as he moved, but he had to make sure they were safe. Soon, Evaine burst through the mouth of the cave and flew sharply upwards to get above the treeline.

"Stay low!" Allard yelled up to her. He didn't know how long she would be able to keep the idea of the griffin in her mind, and didn't want her turning back into a human so high in the sky.

She looked down at him and cocked her head quizzically. He pointed down toward the trees.

Evaine seemed to take his meaning and flew close to the treeline. When Allard saw a clearing in the distance, he yelled again to get Evaine's attention and then pointed at the clearing. Evaine swooped down, landing in the clearing, where she dropped Allard in the tall grass before turning back into a human, tumbling several feet due to the force of her momentum.

They both lurched back up to their feet, though Allard moved a bit slower due to the burn on his ankle. Then they raced toward each other and embraced.

After Allard released Evaine, he reached up and tucked a lock of her dark hair behind her ear. She leaned into the touch before they remembered themselves and pulled apart. Evaine grinned and casually flopped onto her back in the grass.

"We made it!" she said.

Allard didn't answer. He simply focused on putting himself back together. He straightened his mail shirt under his chest plate. He smoothed his hair. He did not look at Evaine.

Evaine lifted her head to try and read Allard's face, but the tall grass obscured her view and she was forced to sit up. "Typically this is where one might respond with a yay, or a huzzah, something in that realm."

"I've got to go back," Allard said. He picked up his sword, wiped the blade on his breeches, and sheathed it. He still didn't look at Evaine. He knew what he would see.

"Back to the dragon's den? The place we just escaped from?" Evaine asked, as she climbed to her feet. She marched over to him, forced him to look at her. If he was leaving to get himself killed, he was going to look her in the eye first.

Allard met her gaze squarely. "Yes."

"You've gone mad," Evaine said.

"I have to." He reached for her hand and she jerked it away.

Evaine nearly screamed at how few words Allard used to speak his own death sentence. But she managed to keep herself under control. there would be time for anger later; for now she needed to convince him to stay. "No. What you have to do is come back with me to the orchard. Hug my little brother hello. And have a meal with my family." Tears welled in Evaine's eyes.

Allard thought about it. He could go back with Evaine. Mila would have cold apple pie. Anders would shake his hand and call him "son" and "my boy". He could sit and tell Layne and the other children stories about the great exploits of heroes gone by. He could kiss Evaine under the apple blossoms and stars.

Except he couldn't.

"I have to do this, Evaine. I have to kill him," Allard said.

"Why?" Evaine cried out. "So you can become king? So your father will acknowledge you as his son? You're not even sure he'll keep to his word. It's not worth your life, Allard!"

After Allard's mother died, he'd been very lonely. Worse, without the queen

84

there to enforce it, many of the servants had gone back to calling him by the wrong name. To combat the pain he felt every time someone misunderstood, purposefully or not, who he was, Allard had developed a little ritual that he'd carried on to adulthood. Whenever he started to doubt himself, or doubt who he was, he would remove a special set of memories from a lovely little box in his mind.

Allard would pore over these memories, holding them up to the light and admiring them as if they were precious stones: the time he had attended the masquerade ball and danced all night with a beautiful girl who'd had no idea who he was. They'd kept their masks on as they kissed under the great staircase in the castle. He remembered when he'd received a gilded horn as the prize for winning his first tournament, the way Dwennon had never ever slipped when addressing him, and every time his father did slip and called him "the boy." Slaying the dragon, having his father acknowledge him: that was to be the crown jewel of the collection. He would finally banish all doubt from the mind of everyone, including himself.

But killing the dragon would not make him any more of a man. If he ran and hid and left this necessary job to someone else, he would still be a man. Even if his father acknowledged him as his son, if he made him king, none of that made him more of a man. He had nothing to prove to his father or anyone else.

Allard was going back because a dragon needed to be slain. Because Balsinew's era of devastation needed to come to an end. Because the question was not whether he was a man, but what kind of man he wanted to be.

Evaine reached out and took Allard's hand. Allard grasped Evaine's hand tightly, then turned her hand so the palm faced upward. He traced the lines of her palm delicately with his fingers, then pressed her hand over her own heart. He left his hand there for a moment, feeling her heart beating.

Allard would have liked to leave his hand resting over Evaine's heart forever, but he removed it, letting his hand instead rest on the pommel of his sword. "I can't let him hurt any more families. Destroy any more villages. I love this kingdom and I won't let one of her largest threats walk free when I can do something about it," Allard said.

Evaine knew she had already lost the battle. If Allard didn't go, didn't fulfill his duty, then it would destroy him. He would never forgive himself. Greatness waited for him. She wouldn't keep him from it.

She slipped the ring off. Allard could feel the metal, still warm from the heat of her hand, as she slid the ring onto his finger.

Then, Evaine ripped the sleeve off the fine royal blue gown the dragon had forced her to wear, which had been obscured by the glass. She smiled at Allard then handed him the sleeve.

"I have no token, but I thought you might wear this into battle," she said.

Allard's eyebrows tilted. For the first time, Evaine saw him smile. a sweet and shy smile, but all that strength underneath. He bowed to her. "Evaine, it would be my honor."

Evaine tied the sleeve around Allard's upper arm. As she did, he told her where her family's horse was tied up. He told her to ride back to her family's orchard as fast as she could. Once he had slain the dragon, he would meet her there.

"You come back," she said.

Allard gently took her hand. He brought it to his lips and kissed it. "Aye, my lady. I shall come back."

Evaine did not allow herself to cry as she watched Allard leave the clearing back toward the dragon's lair. She had to stay steady, she couldn't make him look back with her tears. She needed Allard's mind to be pointing toward the dragon, toward all he needed to do. That was the only way he could come back to her. And she very much needed him to come back, her handsome, quiet prince.

15

Chapter 15

Allard was calm as he entered the cave. He knew what he had to do—he'd been training for this his entire life. He pulled his sword from its sheath. The sword that had been wielded by his father—and mother—his grandfather, great grandfather, great-great grandfather, stretching back for generations to the very first king in their line, the first to be born on a day when the unclouded rains fell. The legacy of his family lived in this blade. He was grateful for the chance to wield it. If he died, he at least knew he would die well. If he succeeded, perhaps he would have his chance to become king. Even if he didn't become king, he would rest easy knowing that he had done all he could to defend the kingdom he loved so much.

When he finally entered the main cavern, Allard found the dragon fretting over the possessions that had been knocked over in the fight. Balsinew was carefully stacking items in elaborate towers to put everything back into its proper place. One of the towers collapsed, and Balsinew roared in frustration as the treasures scattered across the floor of the cave.

Allard moved quietly so as not to waste the element of surprise. He darted across the floor of the cave and ran to the far wall, where a natural rock ledge started near the floor and grew steadily higher until it ended in an overhang right over the dragon's head. Allard climbed this ledge to the top. The dragon was so focused on worrying at his things that he didn't hear the prince creeping above him.

Allard took a deep breath. He would only have one chance to surprise Balsinew while he was distracted restacking the fallen tower of treasure. He had to make it count. And he could not wait—if the dragon moved away from below the ledge then he'd have no advantage at all. Allard dove off the ledge, with both hands wrapped around the hilt of his sword, the blade pointing downward, aiming the sword at Balsinew's skull.

The dragon accidentally knocked over his tower and moved just enough that Allard ended up landing on his back. The dragon shrieked. The sound was tremendous. Balsinew sat up straight, almost like a dog sitting up to beg, his tail whipped the ground. Allard nearly fell off the dragon's back, but he drove the blade through the thick hide between Balsinew's wings. Allard hung there as Balsinew clawed his own back, but his arms were not long enough to reach Allard.

The dragon jumped and bucked, trying to dislodge him. Allard grimly held onto the hilt of his sword, still stuck deep in the dragon's back.

Then Balsinew reared up and staggered backward, intending to crush Allard against the wall. Allard pulled his sword free, sliding down Balsinew's back and tail to the floor of the cavern. He then ran around to the dragon's front and stabbed at Balsinew's belly.

The dragon jetted fire at him, stopped when Allard dove behind a pile of paintings. The dragon refused to damage any of his treasures. When Allard emerged, he held a painting in front of himself like a shield.

Allard rushed at the dragon. Every time the dragon tried to swipe at him with his great claws, Allard brandished the painting at him and the dragon stopped short. Due to the dragon's hesitation, Allard was able to land another blow, drawing more blood, but doing little substantial damage.

The dragon took flight, allowing the wounds Allard had just given him to heal.

Allard took off running toward the long ropes filled with hanging bird cages in the deepest part of the cavern, where it started to narrow and the ceiling was lower. But the dragon didn't follow. For his plan to succeed, Allard had to draw the dragon toward the ropes.

Allard put his hands on one of Balsinew's carefully-crafted towers of treasure. He pushed with all his might, and the tower began to wobble. He pushed again, harder, forcing the tower to list back and forth, back and forth. The wobble grew more pronounced until the tower fell over, knocking over the tower next to it, sending jewels and trinkets and furniture crashing to the floor.

"Stop it!" the dragon snarled, circling in the air above Allard's head.

Allard responded by moving on to another tower. After a bit of effort, that tower toppled over and took down three other towers with it.

The dragon roared in anger. Allard could feel the heat from the fireball gathering in Balsinew's throat, but he knew the dragon would not risk burning his precious trinkets. Balsinew's only options were to sit and wait as Allard destroyed his intricate organization system and his lovely things, or come back down to ground level and fight. Either option suited Allard just fine.

Allard kept knocking over piles of treasure to lead the dragon closer to the ropes holding the birdcages, luring the dragon to his trap.

In front of the birdcages on ropes was a pile of exquisite antique furniture. Allard climbed on top of the pile and began hacking and slashing at the furniture with his sword, snapping off wooden legs, cutting the upholstery to shreds.

Balsinew let out a shriek of impotent rage that forced Allard to pause in his destruction to cover his ears, if only momentarily. The dragon finally returned to the ground. When he landed, the pile of furniture Allard was standing atop shuddered, and Allard nearly fell over. Allard kept his balance and picked his way back down to solid ground on the far side of the mountain of furniture.

The dragon slithered over the top of the pile, barely disturbing the furniture at all, taking special care that his claws did not puncture the delicate upholstery of some of the older pieces. Allard readjusted his position. He'd been expecting the dragon to go around to the side, then he would have been able to attack the dragon's underbelly from below, and continue to drive him toward the ropes, but because the dragon had come over the top, Allard had to stagger backwards or risk getting in range of the dragon's mouth. Balsinew struck at him and Allard stumbled over a chair leg jutting from the mountain. He fell over backwards. The dragon pounced.

The dragon slammed his massive claw on the ground, trying to pin Allard. Allard rolled out of the way and scrambled to his feet. He slashed at the tendons in Balsinew's arm. The dragon screeched and batted him backwards into the cavern wall.

Allard's back slammed into a ledge jutting out from the wall. He crumpled to the ground. For a moment, he couldn't get up. In his mind's eye, Allard saw his father crumpled in the great hall of the castle, unable to protect his wife or children, then his father in his wheelchair, raging at his servants as they tried to help him move from chair to bed. His father would never slay another beast. Allard feared his own fate would be much the same. He had to get up.

Allard rolled onto his side. His ribs, which had likely been merely bruised before, were almost certainly broken. It hurt to move. Hurt to breathe.. His armor had once again taken the brunt of the impact—it was now dented, pressing uncomfortably against his back. He had to get up.

The dragon picked its way toward him.

Allard pushed himself up on his elbow. He had to get up.

He spat into the dirt to clean his teeth of blood. He had to get up.

Allard could see the fireball gathering in the dragon's throat. He had to get up.

Allard rose to one knee. His legs trembled with exhaustion, but he kept moving ever upward. And got up.

He quietly murmured to himself. He only had one option available, and he didn't want the dragon to have any idea what he had planned. He twisted the ring on his finger, maybe it could save him one last time.

Allard limped forward to meet the dragon. Balsinew drew himself up to his full height. He stood up on his hind legs, towering over the prince.

"Well? What are you going to do little prince?" Balsinew asked.

The prince ignored the dragon's taunt, which seemed terribly rude to Balsinew.

The dragon could see the little prince's lips moving, but couldn't make out what he was saying. He assumed the little prince was praying to whatever god little princes prayed to. Or perhaps beseeching his long dead mother to save him. It made little difference.

Balsinew had had enough of this fight. He had grown tired and, though he hated to admit it, afraid. If he had to break a few of his possessions to get rid of this horrible little creature, then that was a price he was finally willing to pay. Things could be replaced. He could even go out and find his Evaine again, once the prince was resting comfortably in his belly.

Balsinew waited for the prince to attack. He would give him quite a surprise when he did. But the prince held. He didn't attack. He just stood there, murmuring to himself.

Well, maybe he'd lost his nerve. Maybe the little prince would be a bit more agreeable now. Maybe Balsinew wouldn't have to kill him. He could keep him. It would be quite lovely to have a matching set. A little prince and a farmer's daughter, both so beautiful. And yet they were very badly behaved. Never had his toys behaved so poorly, at least not since the princeling's mother.

Allard tried every fearsome predator he could think of, wolf and tiger and troll. If this didn't work, he was going to die in this cave. His father would be saddened, but unsurprised. He could almost see the twinkle of pleasure in his brother's black eyes when he was crowned king instead of Allard. Once he was dead, Balsinew would find Evaine and her family again, perhaps he would finally succeed in killing Layne. Allard could not let that happen. He kept trying. Chimera. Boar. Crocodile.

Balsinew dropped his guard, just ever so slightly, perhaps to offer a scolding and a demand to know the whereabouts of Evaine, or at least ask Allard to stop that incessant mumbling.

Then, Allard said the name of one animal sure to defeat Balsinew. He held little faith that it hadn't been taken. But he'd be a fool not to try. "Dragon."

The ground dropped away as Allard rapidly grew taller, until he was only slightly shorter than Balsinew. Where Balsinew was acid green, Allard was golden yellow. His eyes were cold ice blue.

Allard had no idea how long he would be able to hold the idea of the dragon in his mind, and so there was no time for hesitation. Immediately, he clawed at Balsinew's neck. Balsinew moved backward, deeper into the cavern, closer to the ropes. Allard attacked again, snapping his jaws. He took a deep breath, feeling the heat burn at the back of his throat. He opened his jaws and a jet of fire spurted out.

Balsinew tried to dodge it, but the blast of fire caught him full in the chest. He roared and staggered. Allard directed the fire up higher, toward Balsinew's face. The dragon swiped at his face with his claws, trying to protect himself. All the time, he drew closer to the ropes. One of Balsinew's wings brushed against the ropes,the dragon looked backward, taking note for the first time just where he was, and Allard feared that the dragon had figured out his plan.

Balsinew sprang forward, and Allard couldn't react in time, unused as he was to being so large. Balsinew tore into Allard's shoulder, rending the flesh, and Allard roared so loudly it shook the ceiling of the cavern. He clawed at Balsinew's head until Balsinew was forced to let go.

Allard fended off Balsinew's attacks as best he could, but the dragon just kept coming. Some of his wounds were already starting to heal, but just as they finally knitted back together, Balsinew delivered another blow.

Balsinew snapped at him, cobra quick and twice as vicious. He sank his teeth into the soft skin of Allard's side, right below his ribs. Allard tried to get away, but Balsinew would not release Allard. He tore a chunk out of Allard's side. Allard backed off to let the wound heal, blasting intermittent jets of fire to keep Balsinew cornered near the ropes. He glanced down, but the wound had barely healed at all.

Balsinew tried to attack while he was distracted, but Allard caught him in the corner of his eye and spit fire into Balsinew's face, forcing the dragon to retreat.

The wound had healed a bit, but was still bleeding copiously. Allard breathed a wall of fire between himself and Balsinew, continuously feeding it to buy himself a few moments to let the wound heal more. Dwennon had always taught him, if a dragon was overwhelmed, they could fall. And it was looking more likely that Allard would be the one to fall. He would not see Evaine again. He would not see his father's face as he returned to the castle, triumphant. He would not become king.

Balsinew pressed in closer. He would be through the wall soon enough, even if Allard did manage to keep the screen of fire up. Allard needed more time to heal. But he couldn't fly away, because then all his progress driving Balsinew toward the ropes would be for naught. As the wound and Balsinew's continuous attacks wore Allard down, the wall weakened and Balsinew burst through. Allard had to return to the fight, whether he was ready or not.

Balsinew took advantage of Allard's weakened state to bat him to the ground. He clawed at Allard, but Allard was able to roll out of the way, knocking over several towers of treasure, and bending one of his wings backwards uncomfortably. Balsinew hooked his claws into Allard's side and dragged him backward, aiming for better access to Allard's vulnerable throat.

Allard grabbed at one of the towers of treasure and sent it crashing down on top of Balsinew, distracting the dragon long enough for Allard to get himself righted. The prince swiped at Balsinew with his great claws and sent the dragon flying into the ropes. Balsinew thrashed and writhed, but only succeeded in getting himself tangled in the ropes, until they were hopelessly twisted and snarled around his wings. The dragon tried to take off into flight and crashed to the ground.

Allard lunged for Balsinew but Balsinew sent a fireball hurtling straight for him. It punched through Allard's wing. Allard roared in pain, he could feel the blackened flesh of the thin membrane of his wing still smoldering.

With Allard distracted, Balsinew jetted small bursts of fire through his nostrils, trying to burn the ropes away. He burned away the one wrapped around his neck, twisting this way and that in order to singe the rope without burning himself. The ropes slid down to the floor. Balsinew lifted his head as much as he could to burn the next few further down his body.

Allard could not let the dragon escape. If Balsinew managed to get free, Allard would never get him contained again. He was too weak, he wouldn't be able to hold the idea of the dragon in his mind for much longer.

Allard pounced on top of Balsinew, tipping him over backward, pinning him on his back, clawing at his neck and chest. Balsinew flailed about but was wrapped too tight to right himself or fight back much. Allard was about to deal the killing blow when he lost the idea of the dragon in his mind. The world grew larger as he grew smaller.

Most of Allard's wounds had healed, but the deep gouge on his side still had not knitted together completely, and it remained when he returned to his human form. He used the blade of his sword to remain standing on top of the uneven landscape of the dragon's body where he stood. The very tip of the blade sank into the dragon's hide, but not enough to do any damage, for that, Allard would need to reach the dragon's heart.

Balsinew's body seemed to stretch out forever from Allard's vantage point atop the dragon's fish-white belly.

Balsinew twisted and bucked, doing his best to throw Allard off his body. But Allard moved relentlessly forward. He clutched at his side with one hand and carried his father's black-bladed sword, forged with the metal of a fallen star, in the other, racing to the dragon's heart.

The dragon panicked and sent bursts of flame shooting wildly into the air. A few flames got close to Allard, but not so close that he even bothered to duck. The dragon thrashed and floundered, anything to slow the prince's progress.

Finally, Allard stood on the dragon's chest. Balsinew's chest rose up and down as the dragon's breathing grew panicked. Allard could feel the dragon's heart beating under his feet.

All the dragon could do was watch. Fear caused his glittering green eyes to lose some of their sparkle.

Allard raised his sword over his head. He looked the dragon in the eye and said, "This is for my mother." Then he plunged his sword into the dragon's heart.

Balsinew screeched and shrieked. He shuddered and convulsed. Then, the great ball of fire in the back of his throat went out, and the dragon was dead.

16

Chapter 16

Allard slid down the dragon's side and watched to make sure the dragon was dead. When he had determined the dragon was truly gone, all of Allard's remaining strength vanished and he dropped to his knees. Wrung out and weak, he had to hang off his sword to remain upright. The only sound in the entire cavern was his breathing. All was quiet. He'd done it.

After a few moments, during which he gathered his strength, Allard rose to his feet. He walked to the dragon's head and pried open the dragon's massive eyelid. He used his sword to pop out Balsinew's glittering eye, still a vivid dancing green, his proof that he had done what he set out to do. It remained to be seen whether his father would keep his word. He didn't allow himself to think about it.

Allard moved more and more slowly as blood seeped through his mail shirt and dripped to the dirt. He searched for a moment and found a bag large enough to carry the eye, then slung the bag across his back, sheathed his sword, and made his way out of the dragon's lair.

Allard emerged, blinking into the late afternoon sunlight. His hair was a sweaty mess, his chest plate had a deep claw mark down the front. He still wore the sleeve Evain had tied around his arm, though it was so bloodstained as to be nearly unrecognizable.

"Allard!" a voice called.

Allard looked toward the source of the voice. It was Evaine, who emerged from the rocky outcropping where she'd been hiding, because, of course, she had not listened to him, of course, she'd needed to make sure he was alright. Allard smiled, took two steps forward, then collapsed, disappearing in the tall grass that surrounded the entrance to the cave.

"Allard!" Evaine screamed. She ran up the hill, nearly tripping on the hem of the blue ball gown she was wearing.

Finally, she reached where he had fallen, face down, unconscious. There was blood all over the grass. Evaine turned Allard on his side so she could better see his wound. She pulled up his mail shirt; a vicious bite tore into his lower back up toward his ribs.

Evaine tore off her other sleeve. She used the sleeve to staunch the blood. The most important thing was to get the bleeding stopped. She needed to stitch him up.

Evaine prayed that the spool of unicorn hair thread was still in his pocket. It wasn't in the pocket on the right side, near the wound on Allard's side. She gently rolled him on his back so she could reach his other pocket.

Allard moaned in pain. Evaine quickly brushed his hair out of his face.

"I'm sorry," she whispered. "You'll be alright in a moment."

She pulled the spool of thread from his pocket and nearly cried with relief. Then she quickly threaded the needle and set to work stitching Allard back together again. His skin knitted together quickly wherever she laid a stitch. But he was still deathly pale.

Finally, she had closed all of his wounds and they were healing at a rapid pace. But Allard still hadn't woken up.

Evaine gently patted his cheek. "Allard. Please wake up. Please."

Tears drifted down Evaine's cheeks in little tributaries. She leaned down and kissed Allard's forehead. Then she sat down, letting the ballgown pool around her, and laid Allard's head in her lap. There was nowhere to go. There was nothing else to do. She ran her fingers through Allard's hair and waited for him to wake up.

Allard felt warm sunlight play across his face. He felt strong fingers playing through his hair. At first he couldn't remember where he was, or what had happened. But a dull pain radiated from his side, reminding him of the fight with the dragon, reminding him of his victory. He blinked slowly and saw a pair of beautiful brown eyes staring down at him.

"Evaine.." His voice was a low painful bark. He coughed, clearing the smoke and blood from his raw throat.

"So you remember me. No damage to your brains, then," Evaine said, trying to make a joke.

Allard sat up and wrapped his arms around her, pulling her into a tight embrace. He pulled back until his cheek pressed against hers. They breathed each other in. But Allard had to break the moment. He winced and turned away; his side was mostly healed, but still a bit tender.

He pulled up the side of his mail shirt and looked down at the stitches Evaine had laced into his side. "These are a bit sloppy. Who taught you to sew?" he asked, hoping to catch her off guard enough to make her laugh. He was rewarded when Evaine's eyes crinkled up and a hearty laugh spilled from her lips.

Evaine hid her eyes with her hand for a moment, covering her laugh, before sneering at him playfully. "Oh, and I suppose you could have done better?"

"I could have actually. I'm quite good at sewing," Allard said. Then he laughed as well.

Evaine didn't think she'd ever heard a sound so beautiful as Allard laughing, all the more wonderful for how rare it was. It started low in his chest, as if he was reluctant to let it escape. It was hesitant, as if he still really wasn't sure he was doing the right thing by letting go of his hard fought stoicism. But when he finally got going, his laughter was so joyful and open. Evaine was determined to make Allard laugh at every opportunity, so she would never forget what his laughter sounded like.

Their laughter twined together, her voice taking the high road, his, the low. Eventually, the laughter did not die, so much as fade away to comfortable silence. It was time to go home.

Evaine helped Allard to his feet. Allard slowly and painfully climbed onto her family's horse. He pulled Evaine up behind him. They rode back toward her family's orchard with Evaine clinging to Allard's back, with her arms wrapped around his waist and her chin hooked over his shoulder.

Slowly, the forest trees thinned out and gave way to apple trees. As they got closer to the house, Evain saw 5 little faces pressed to the window. There was a great racket as the children raced toward the door.

"Evaine's back! Evaine's back!"

Allard dismounted. He would have liked to have lifted Evaine from the saddle and lowered her gently to the ground, as he would easily be able to do if he was uninjured, but he had to settle for offering her a hand as she jumped down by herself.

All of the children ran out of the house, closely followed by their parents. Anders quickly outpaced his children and his wife, racing to Evaine and picking her up to swing her around in a circle. After a moment, he sat her down so her mother could cover her face in kisses. Then all of the children wrapped their arms around her.

Allard allowed Evaine to have her reunion in peace. He walked unsteadily over to the tree where he'd put on his armor just a few hours ago. He braced his back against the tree and sank down with his legs splayed in front of him. He took a deep breath, found that it was good—less painful than before—and decided to take another. Maybe he would just close his eyes for a moment...

Layne was the first to break away from the reunion. He ran over and hugged Allard, causing the prince's eyes to fly open in surprise before he returned the hug. The rest of the children followed, burying Allard in a fond dogpile. It was a lucky thing the unicorn hair had done its work.

"You did it!" Layne yelled. "I knew you would."

Then Anders came over, dug Allard out from the pile of children, and pumped Allard's hand up and down. "Thank you, son. Thank you for bringing both of my children back to me."

Then Mila came over and kissed Allard's cheek. "Thank you." She helped Allard to his feet and led him into the little farm house. He protested weakly, but she insisted he needed rest.

Allard was able to sleep for approximately 45 minutes before Layne came in and began bouncing on his bed, demanding to know how Allard had defeated the dragon, if he could show Layne the eyeball, and if Allard was going to marry Evaine.

That night, the family invited Allard to dine with them in the orchard. Layne's older brothers helped the younger children string lanterns through the apple trees. Anders and Mila set up the table, while Allard and Evaine guiltily watched without helping. They'd both tried to insinuate themselves into the preparations several times and had been roundly rebuked.

They ate under the soft glow of the lanterns, with the scent of hearty food and apple blossoms hanging in the air. Evaine and Allard recounted their adventure with the dragon, though Evaine was more the natural storyteller. Allard loved the way she spoke with her hands and did voices and made exaggerated faces. He was content to just watch her tell the story. When they finally reached the part of the story he had to tell alone, the part where Allard had actually slain the dragon, the entire family turned their attention to him with expectant eyes.

"After I parted with Evaine, I returned to the cavern, and slayed the dragon," Allard said.

"But how?" Layne asked.

"I stabbed him with my sword," Allard said.

The entire family stared at him again, entreating him to continue with their eyes.

"But *how?*" Layne asked, he was familiar with Allard's rather dry storytelling style from their time in the cave, but Allard had slain a *dragon*, surely there was more to the story.

Allard looked at Evaine for help. She reached out and patted his arm. Mila and Anders noted this and smiled at each other.

Evaine had managed to drag a few details out of Allard on the ride home, and so she was able to spin the events into a proper tale. Once she was done, she turned to Allard and whispered in his ear, "We'll work on it, for next time." It was the story of how they met, after all.

Eventually, the children were all sent to bed. And soon, Evaine's parents followed suit, giving Evaine and Allard a kiss and a hug each.

Evaine led Allard deep into the orchard. Fireflies danced in the darkness. They held hands. She talked and he laughed. Then they stood under the oldest tree in the orchard. And he kissed her under the apple blossoms.

Then he whispered in her ear, "Can I come back? To court you?"

She giggled a bit at his formality, already quite dear to her. "I'd be furious if you didn't."

The man she loved let out a sigh of relief as if the matter had truly been in question. Then he kissed her again. And again. And again.

17

Chapter 17

T he next morning, Allard prepared to go back through the tunnel, with the flower Wendla had given him. Hopefully, this time he would not encounter any unexpected guests. He had to go home, to claim what was his.

Allard said goodbye to Mila and Anders and the rest of the children. He kissed Evaine goodbye. All of Evaine's siblings, except for Layne, giggled into their hands. Layne remained stoically above such nonsense. Mila and Anders pretended not to see. Evaine's parents knew the young ones were breaking etiquette by kissing so soon after meeting, but they also knew a little something about love at first sight.

Allard knelt down and held out his arms so that he could hug Layne.

Layne buried his face in Allard's shoulder. "You're going to come back right?"

Allard smiled. "Oh yes, I wager you'll be sick of me soon enough."

Layne looked up at him very seriously. "No I won't."

"Well, that's good," Allard said. "Because I spoke with your parents, and they've agreed—once you're a bit older, you can be my squire. If you'd like."

Allard once again held his breath as if the matter were in some doubt.

Layne screeched in excitement, "yes yes yes yes." He gave Allard another tremendous hug.

"I'll be back soon," Allard said. Then he lifted the leather cord, from which hung the bottle of Water of the Cave-mers over his head, and handed it to Layne. There was only a tiny bit left. "I want you to have this. In case you ever find yourself in the dark again."

He hugged Layne again, slung the bag with Balsinew's eye across his back and walked to the mouth of the tunnel. He collected a message from Maurice to deliver to Wendla and entered the tunnel with enough torches to see him through and the flower pinned over his heart.

Before, the journey had taken all day and all night, but without the tunnel working on his mind, the journey only took a few hours. He emerged from the tunnel, blinking in the strong sunlight. Eventually his eyes adjusted and he could see Wendla's little farm. He climbed the steps he'd repaired to reach her front door and knocked.

Allard gave Wendla her flower, her message, and a hug. Then, he collected Ondine and the rest of his belongings and moved ever onward.

They rode for days, he and Ondine, making short work of the Upside Down Lake and the Prism Valley. The sand from his first journey through had not shifted and so he was able to find safe passage with little incident. When he next came to visit Evaine, he intended to map the valley. He also planned to ask Dwennon to find another flower like Wendla's. He couldn't, in good conscience, keep borrowing hers. It had to grow somewhere and if anyone could find it, it would be Dwennon.

Before long, he found himself on roads he had known all his life, recognizing every house and tree.

Allard reached the outer wall of the castle. The gigantic doors opened for him and he rode Ondine through them. He rode Ondine up the bridge to the main part of the castle. He rode her through the hallway leading to the throne room, drawing stares from servants and members of the court. A small child pointed at the bloodstained sack on his back and asked her mother loudly what it was. The child's mother shushed her and pulled her back toward the exit to the castle.

Allard's face remained wooden but his hands shook as he approached the door to the throne room. He carefully dismounted Ondine. He petted her face and then wrapped his arms around her neck. "Thank you, lovely girl," he murmured so only she could hear. He left her in the hallway, he knew she would be waiting for him, no matter what happened next.

Allard stood in front of the door. He set back his shoulders and straightened his clothes. Now, he would find out if he was to be king. He threw open the doors and strided into the great throne room.

There his father sat, hearing the petitions of his subjects. Braxton sat at his right hand, slouched over in his gilded chair, bored. But he sat up quickly when he recognized the person in the doorway.

The throne room was dead silent as Allard walked the length of the room to reach the dais where his brother and father sat. His footsteps echoed in the great hall. But for once, the sound did not intimidate him. There would be no ducking his head, no scurrying, no hand wringing—desperately trying to think of some way, any way, to please his father. Finally, he stopped in front of the dais and met his father's gaze.

Allard pulled the eye out of the bag and held it up for all to see. "I did as I said I would. I have brought you the glittering eye of Balsinew."

King Cederic's brow softened momentarily, but he adopted a more neutral expression.

Braxton straightened up, his face pulled into a sneer. "That could belong to anyone," he said at the same time the king said, "You're home."

Allard handed the eye to a guard, so that he might take it up to the king. The king only gave it a cursory glance, he passed it back to the guard, and focused all his attention on Allard.

Braxton snatched the eye out of the guard's hands, examining it fiercely.

For the second time that day, the doors of the great hall were dramatically thrown open. Allard looked back to see Dwennon standing in the doorway. Dwennon rushed into the throne room. "I saw you coming up the bridge." Dwennon, who had rarely struggled to summon a word in his life, was at a loss. All he could do was rush forward and grip Allard's forearm, as Allard did the same. They pressed their foreheads together. Then Dwennon hugged Allard. "I am so proud of you. You did it. You're going to be king."

Allard let go of Dwennon. He cast his eye upon his father. "Am I, Father? Am I going to be king?"

Allard had spent so much of his life trying to please this man, trying to prove that he was worthy, trying to prove that he was a man, despite not being born one. But that meant little to him now. He knew what he was, who he was, and what he was meant to do. He was meant to rule this kingdom he loved so much.

Allard awaited his father's answer.

King Cederic looked upon his child. He remembered the raindrop tapping his forehead on a cloudless day, how happy he'd been, because he'd been given a son. He had thought the prophecy had gotten it wrong, that the cosmos had made a mistake. But it was he, the King, who had made the mistake.

Allard had done what the king could never do, avenged the death of his wife, Allard's mother. The king had always seen so much of Belinda in their son, her kindness, her bravery, her unswerving dedication to the kingdom. But for the first time the king saw something of himself in Allard, *his*—Cederic's—fierceness, *his* honor, *his* strength. He saw these things, because Allard was his son, and rightful heir to the throne.

The king gestured for Allard to kneel. He did so. Then he tipped his eyes up, asking the question one more time.

"Yes, my son. You will be king," Cederic said.

Allard ducked his head down and allowed a small smile to cross his face, but that was all. By the time he arose, his face was once again set. "Thank you, father," Allard said.

Perhaps the king had hoped his eldest son would race forward and embrace him, smile upon him with the warmth he shared with that wiley old wizard pretending to be an etiquette teacher, tell him of all his travels and adventures. They would talk late into the night about all that needed to be done.

But the prince did none of these things, and the king knew it was his own fault. He had waited too long. Perhaps in time things might improve. But then again, he did not have much time left. Death's cruelest trick was giving you the wisdom to see your mistakes and too little time to do anything about it.

A few weeks later, the king laid in his deathbed. He and Allard had spent much time together, as he prepared his oldest boy to lead, as he should have done all along. But now he was nearly gone.

After Allard told the king what Braxton had done, sending the bandits after him, Cederic had Braxton confined to his room, with armed guards posted. But Allard told the king he would want to see Braxton before he died, and so Braxton was allowed to come to his quarters.

Braxton entered the room to find Allard sitting at his father's right side, his face buried in his hands. He straightened up when he finally heard Braxton's footsteps. His eyes were red and his face was wet. His short hair stood up in a cowlick in front.

Braxton flopped down into the chair on their father's other side. "What are you crying about? We knew he was dying. And you didn't even like him," Braxton asked.

Allard stared at him, wondering how one could be so callous. But he saw the genuinely confused look on Braxton's face and realized that his brother was asking a legitimate question. He legitimately did not understand why Allard could possibly be so upset.

"Because this is as good as we will ever be," Allard said. And it was far too little, far too late. He slowly reached out and took his father's hand. "It's not fair that I have to forgive you so quickly."

His father's lips moved but no sound came out.

Allard kissed his father's hand. "I'll take good care of her. I'll keep the kingdom safe."

King Cederic the Slayer of the Sea Beast died knowing that his kingdom was in good hands, that his boy would rule with kindness and wisdom, that he would gladly lie down his life to protect it, and he would always love it.

Braxton slowly rose to his feet. "The king is dead. Long live the king."

With that, Braxton swept out of the room. He didn't want to imagine what Allard had planned for him, now that their father couldn't protect him anymore. Surely, he would put Braxton on the rack or in the iron maiden. It is what Braxton would have done had their roles been reversed, and he would have taken great pleasure in it. He fled by nightfall. Allard never saw him again.

Bells rang throughout the kingdom on the day of King Allard's coronation.

In the orchard, the bells rang only for the trees, as Evaine, Layne, and the rest of the family had been invited to the coronation as the king's special guests. Wendla rang a bell of her own, disturbing the quiet in her little acre of paradise, a bright smile on her face. The bells followed Braxton as he slinked from pub to tavern, town to town, fleeing though no one chased him.

Eventually, the new king's most trusted advisor, Dwennon, was able to find Allard a flower, just like Wendla's, so that he might more easily visit his love and her family, who quickly became his family as well. Allard and Evaine married in the summer. She was a good queen. She understood the will of the people better than any member of Allard's court, and she was quite good at making him laugh.

King Allard acquired many honorifics throughout his long rule. The first was Allard the Dragon Slayer. His last was Allard of the Hundred Year Rule, after he died on the 100 year anniversary of his coronation.

The skies opened up and rained on a cloudless day to mourn the passing of the king, who was not born a man, but became one through force of will and purity of heart. King Allard the Brave. The Wise. The Kind. Monster Slayer. Map Maker. Father to a Kingdom. Eldest Son of an Eldest Son. And King of the Realm.

THE END

Acknowledgments

Publishing a book has long been a dream of mine. I started my first "novel" when I was in the fifth grade and I've been writing ever since. So, I am unbelievably excited to finally publish my first actual honest to God book.

I want to thank my mom, for always encouraging me to put my stuff out there, being my first reader, and just for being a great mom in general.

I want to thank my fourth grade teacher, Mrs. Fairfield, for being the first person to tell me I was a good writer.

Thank you to Cassandra Faustini for being an amazing editor and putting up with just a ridiculous amount of sentence fragments.

Thank you to Matthew Smaglik, one of my best friends and occasional writing partner, for being an awesome sounding board and always pushing me to go beyond the easy first idea.

And finally, thank you to everyone who has read my work over the years, offering encouragement, feedback, and quoting stuff I wrote back to me, it never ever gets old.

Made in the USA
Coppell, TX
05 March 2021

51324084R00069